To you
with best
wishes,

Chris

2014.

KARL AND THE KILLER'S KISS

Other books by Christopher John:

The Legend of J.C. Holmes
Peter Fry at Exit 30
Savage
Hoodoo

Karl and the
Killer's Kiss

Christopher John

UNITED WRITERS
Cornwall

UNITED WRITERS PUBLICATIONS LTD
Ailsa, Castle Gate, Penzance, Cornwall.

British Library Cataloguing in Publication Data:
A catalogue record for this book is
available from the British Library.

ISBN 1 85200 103 8

Printed in Great Britain by
United Writers Publications Ltd
Cornwall.

To Mum, Alison and Katy.

Special thanks to Joyce
for the typing.

Chapter One

"Guilty!"

The judge tilted back his head. "That is the verdict of you all?"

"It is."

Karl involuntarily quailed as the judge's face swivelled from the foreman of the jury to himself.

"Karl Lawrence you have been found guilty of the heinous murder of three women. They trusted you, lavished their affection upon you, and you cold-bloodedly murdered them."

Karl opened his mouth to protest but nothing came out.

"It is my duty to remove you permanently from the society of decent men and particularly women. I sentence you to 25 years imprisonment and I recommend you serve the full term. Take him down."

Despair gripped Karl: to be plunged into a black hole of a cell for the rest of his life. Never to roam the countryside free again, never to love.

He shook off the invading hands. "Get off me, you bastards no, no . . . I won't, stop!"

"It's all right."

"What?"

Still the hands, shaking him, rousing him, lifting him.

"Your tea."

"What? Pardon?"

"I've brought you your tea. I do wish they'd use the proper stuff, not tea bags."

Puzzled, Karl rubbed his eyes in disbelief.

"Tea," Jardine, his barrister pointed to his mug on the bare table in front of him. "Drink it, it'll make you feel better. Here, are you all right? You look all greenish round the gills."

Coming round, Karl nodded, and sipped his tea.

What a time to drop off! The strain must have finally told on him. The barrister sniffed. "They'll be out for ages yet."

Jardine looked down at his seated client and wondered at his chances. He looked personable in his grey double-breasted worsted suit with the white shirt and blue striped tie. Almost too personable with his high cheek-boned good looks, which women found irresistible. Those on the jury couldn't take their eyes off him, but did that mean they thought him incapable of murder? Probably. The men on the jury mistrusted him – 'too good looking by half', 'fancies himself', 'a lady killer'?

"Give me a cigarette will you?" Karl hadn't smoked for ages but was desperate for one now.

Jardine obliged with a packet he kept specially.

"Why are they taking so long?" Karl railed. Here he was, in the bowels of the court, down endless flights of stairs where the air was dank. And way up above his future was being weighed in the balance.

Angela Monks, 41, strangled; Joan Devizes, 38, bludgeoned to death; Fiona Strang, 40, stabbed twelve times. How could they think it was him? He'd been fond of all these women, loved them in his casual way: not sponged off them and killed them the way the prosecution had made out.

Unless – and then that tiny pinpoint of horror, that devil's eye opened as he glimpsed a possibility. High on ecstasy and cocktails of drugs after an all-night acid house rave, could he have done any of these murders then blanked it out? He had memory gaps after raves, and the magic rituals he indulged in. It was all a mixed up confusion.

He was sweating now, clenching and unclenching his fists, and then banging them on the table till Jardine pressed a hand on his shoulder. No, no – it still wasn't him. He had no urge to kill: he loved women or at least wanted them insatiably. Love perhaps was beyond him. It seemed to require communication, tenderness in which he was lacking. All he wanted to do was to lose himself with a woman for a while.

To break into his own chain of thoughts he turned to Jardine: "What are my chances?" His face was anguished.

Jardine, tall, with shiny hair, aquiline, viewed his client coolly, dispassionately. "Good, I should think. You made a fine

8

impression in court, just the way I coached you. Not cocky but shy, sincere, distraught. And the prosecution's case was wholly circumstantial: it all boiled down to the fact that as their lover you were the one link between these three women. If only you could have been more certain with your alibis."

Karl heartily agreed. But considering he had been so out of his head these last few months, remembering which day it was had been a challenge. And then there were those gaps in his memory – those voids where anything might have happened.

What Jardine hoped, but didn't say, was that Karl's whole life story and reputation hadn't reached the jury. Casanova, jack-the-lad, was maybe acceptable; but what about the background of deceased criminal father, the mother who had deserted him as a child, the wild youth spent in children's homes, then petty theft, the grudge against all policemen. There was the illegal whisky still, the pirate radio and raves held in the hills, the dabbling in the occult, the ecstasy . . . no, it was fervently to be hoped all of this hadn't reached the jury's ears. If it had . . . his client was cooked.

Karl stared up, suddenly angry at being appraised. He had his feelings: grief and sorrow over those deaths, women he had loved in his fashion. People thought he lived off them as a toy boy, or a male prostitute, but it wasn't true. He'd liked them all, lavished presents on them when he could, anything to give them pleasure. And now they were dead.

Why older women? Because they made less demands, were so kind, so understanding, so warm.

Like Gloria, mane of black hair, great gold bands on her arms, in a long billowing dress railing at the police to let her see him.

Was she to be the next murder victim? The next link in that obscene chain linked to him?

No, that must never happen. He'd die first. Or rot in prison, as he had been doing all these months on remand, until he thought he'd go mad.

He needed the hills to wander, and from his secret cave to drink illicit whisky and watch the deer.

Please, he prayed eyes closed, let it be over soon. Then he heard a whispering in the corner of the room nearest the door.

He opened his eyes.

Jardine nodded. "They're ready for us."

Chapter Two

Eager, inquisitive spectators strained for a good look at him as Karl was led back to the dock.

He tried to read the face of the foreman of the jury but it was inscrutable, merely lined, tired, relieved that the whole ordeal of judgement was over.

The judge inclined his head. "Have you reached a verdict upon which you are all agreed?"

The foreman rose. "We have."

The judge then proceeded through the three counts of murder.

Karl stood rigid, as if paralysed, his face taut, angular, staring ahead at nothing.

"Not guilty."

"Not guilty."

"Not guilty."

The foreman's firm voice rapped out the verdict.

A great gasp went up in the court; of surprise, disbelief, amazement. There was joy in some quarters, dark mutterings in others, admiration for Karl – and disgust.

Karl listened but found it hard to take it in. The judge was telling him he was a free man, free to go but he couldn't move. Remand and the trial had so taken over his life, he couldn't believe it was over, couldn't imagine any other life but arresting officers, endless interrogations, cells, court rooms.

Then Gloria rushed over to him, a smile from ear to ear, and grabbed his arm before anyone else could.

"Well done, I knew it. They'd never convict you, a good boy like you. One look told them you were innocent."

She smothered him with kisses, pressed his face against her.

He smelt that familiar heady orange blossom perfume, and felt those bangles as her arms closed around him.

Then she was taking him by the hand and dragging him at a run from the dock. "Come on Karl, the party starts here."

He flushed and then let out a whoop and a yell. Suddenly all the cramped pain of being the accused fell away and he realised his own acquittal, his own freedom.

Uncaring he ran with her full tilt down the aisle of the court as bystanders scrambled for a closer look and camera men closed in.

Then they both had to pull up hard as the prosecuting police slowly filed out, blocking the way.

Detective Randle, a gnarled middle-aged loner, embittered, unsociable and resentful, glared at Karl.

"So you got away with it, used your pretty-boy looks on these women jurors. Well you cut no ice with me. I'm sick of watching guilty men like you walk away. I've had a bellyful."

And he stomped off to find the nearest bar, a prickly, overweight figure. No one dared or wanted to follow him.

Angry at the scene and the delay, Gloria bawled after him, "Nutcase," and then dragged Karl round the clogged huddle of policemen and out onto the courtroom steps.

Then Karl stopped her. He stood apart and took in the air, watched the pigeons swooping out of the sky, looked up at the fathomless blue.

"I'm out and I'm free. I can do anything I like, no one can stop me. Yippee!" He let out a huge, incongruous, cowboy yodel.

Gloria laughed and shouted out with him. Arms round each other's waists they bowled down the steps and headed for Gloria's sports car.

Her gleaming vintage MG stood unclamped on double yellow lines.

"You must be mad," Karl told her.

"Mustn't I just," and she winked at him. " Let's go," she called out, as a traffic warden began bearing down on them.

She let in the clutch and the car rocketed away, narrowly missing a lurching delivery van.

"Road hog," and Gloria blasted her horn.

All the way out of town she regaled him with her plans, the celebrations they were going to have, and how they were going to make up for lost time. "You ought to sue for wrongful

11

imprisonment," she rounded off.

"That I should. Those bastards were out to get me, just 'cos I'd known all those women at one time or another. Not that any of them could hold a candle to you."

Gloria laughed. "You don't have to explain to me. So you've put it about a bit. I'm broad-minded provided you come back to me – for the main meal." Her eyes gleamed in anticipation. She'd had a special four-poster bed installed.

Now they were hurtling down the huge incline which led to the village. Giant boulders stood on either side and then below rocks lay scattered like playthings.

The car juddered over cattle grids and spun dangerously on bends. Then they were coasting down into the one main village street.

Karl had half imagined bunting, and 'Welcome Home' banners draped about, assembled villagers beaming their joy, but instead nothing. Not one person was to be seen. It was like a ghost town.

Even Gloria's mood was dampened and she became uneasy, slowing the car. Further down they encountered a flock of sheep crossing the road to pasture, led by a man in worn breeches and a formless hat.

"Look who I've got here Oswald," called out Gloria, but Oswald didn't turn his head and carried on the same shambling plod.

"Oswald, you hear me well and good so don't turn your back on me," Gloria rounded on him.

At that Oswald stopped, seemed to pause to ruminate, and then turned. "You should never have brought that murdering swine back here. We all know what he did. Hanging's too good for him. So get rid of him if you know what's good for you."

"But he's been found innocent. Damn it, he is innocent, you all know that surely." Gloria was exasperated.

"Do we?" Oswald leered at her. "Quite the contrary," he countered, suddenly loquacious. "Listen, we knew and loved every one of his victims. Born and bred here they were. We won't let him get away with it."

Angry, Gloria hit the horn and accelerated round the shepherd and his flock. "I'd like to run him and his damn sheep down."

She was heartily glad to put him, and the silent, uneasy village street behind her as she headed them up to her house on the rise.

Gloria's home was a spacious bungalow in contrast to the drystone cottages which formed the majority of the village. She led him by the hand through the vestibule, then playfully told him to close his eyes.

Doing as he was told he stumbled forward till Gloria shouted, "Tarra, tarra," mimicking a fanfare.

Karl opened his eyes with delight: a banner was draped across the room spelling out, 'Welcome Back Karl'. Behind, a trestle table groaned with a profusion of bottles, cold buffet, and gateau.

All that was missing were people.

"Come on, have a drink. By God you deserve one," and Gloria passed him a bottle of champagne.

Rapidly Karl had the cork popped and the frothing liquid into two glasses. Then he was slurping it happily, uncaring for niceties. "Gloria, I could hug you. What a welcome!"

"Then why don't you?"

And then they had a clumsy embrace, trying not to spill their glasses. Their lips smacked together then became glued.

"Oi, you two, that's enough of that," a voice said jovially. "I want a share."

Karl and Gloria turned to see Judy advancing ahead of Sarah: Gloria's grown-up daughters.

Judy was poured into a smooth black halter dress that seemed to swim over her perfect figure like a dark river. Her green eyes shone under dark curved eyebrows.

Reluctantly Gloria made way for her brash daughter who fell into Karl's arms and smothered his mouth with luscious warm kisses.

"Remember how good those are?" Judy teased him.

Gloria was a shade off becoming blazing mad.

A gentle arm was placed on her shoulder to calm her. Sarah wore a peach apron dress which revealed sensually shaped arms and legs, and a perfectly oval face with hazel eyes which in a moment could turn from demure and innocent into alluring pools. Whereas both Gloria and Judy had dark black hair, Sarah's was a deep chestnut swept back from her face.

When even Judy seemed to have had her fill and was left gazing into Karl's eyes, while caressing his hair, Sarah smoothed a path in.

"My turn I think," she said quietly, and wrapped Karl around

13

her breathing huskily: "Welcome home."

Judy and Gloria exchanged glances which said, 'sly devil'.

Other friends then made their entrance from the kitchen but still the party was pitifully small.

"Where is everybody?" Judy demanded.

Gloria looked up from refilling her glass. "If you mean the villagers, it's a boycott."

"A what? After Karl's release and everything?"

"Yes. How people could still believe such terrible things about our Karl after he's been ex . . . exonerated," came out mangled.

"Well let's not talk about that," Sarah intervened, keen to smooth it over. "I'm sure Karl wants to forget."

Karl said nothing. At this present moment forget: yes. But later he'd remember, those poor women he'd loved. It was tragic. Under the influence of the champagne he suddenly felt like crying.

"I'm sure he does." A loud man's voice came from the front doorway. Detective Randle stumbled in, obviously well oiled already.

"I wouldn't have missed this shindig for the world. I want to see how a murderer celebrates getting off the hook."

Gloria pushed forward. "No one invited you, gate-crashing a private party. Go on, clear off, or I'll have you thrown out. Making evil drunken accusations."

"Hark at you," Randle called back, "you old bag. Cradle snatcher. With your toy boy killer here. You must be very proud."

"Right, that's it," and Gloria launched herself, fists flying, at Randle.

But Karl was too quick for her and spinning Randle round dragged him into the garden to cool off.

Suddenly Randle gagged, and bent full over before slowly recovering himself. Then he stood up and wiped his mouth on his sleeve. He scowled at Karl. "Do you know what you and your kind have cost me? Ruining my health working eighteen hours a day and for what? To get you banged to rights and then see you walk away."

Randle uttered the deepest embittered sigh and stumbled about the rockery as if looking for something he'd lost.

"I've had it up to here. Do you know how long I've been on the force? Twenty bloody years and only made sergeant. Can you believe it? Twenty years of my life given. Umpteen arrests, commendations, clean record and what to show for it? Sergeant. I ask you. So you go on and have a good laugh. One of us is the real mug."

Karl waited for Randle to calm down. "I'm not laughing."

"Aren't you, well you should be. Beat the rap as our American cousins say. But do you know something, I'll nail you if it's the last thing I do."

Karl eyed him steadily. "You really want to get something on me, don't you? Prove I did those murders?"

"Sure, sure. But then there's no point, is there? You can't be tried twice for the same crime."

"But for your own satisfaction?"

Even Randle, bleary from drink could tell something strange was on offer. "What are you driving at?"

"I'll offer a reward – £10,000 – to anyone who can discover who killed them."

Randle stared at him as if he was mad. "You killed them, so what are you trying to pull?"

"I want to know the truth. There's a psychotic killer out there and I want him stopped."

Randle laughed harshly. "You did it, but you want to shift the blame. That's all."

"Believe that if you want to. But you know more about this case than anyone. You can have the reward if you find the killer."

Randle looked him up and down in disgust. "Oh yes, I'd like to take your money but only to prove that you killed those women in cold blood. Then maybe you'd do the right thing and kill yourself."

Randle stopped unsteadily, pulling a half bottle of scotch from his stained overcoat pocket.

He took a swig, emptied it, then hurled it without looking into the ditch by the side of the road.

Chapter Three

Karl watched Randle go with mixed emotions: pity, vague hope that he'd find the killer, and also distrust for the man who tried so hard to convict him. But who else should he confide in? Who else knew so much about the case, without having to start again from scratch?

Then again for the umpteenth time since the acquittal he asked himself, why was he doing this? Why not put it behind him, forget it like a bad dream.

But those poor dead women: who would remember their fate if not him? And what about the others who might be dying right now because no one had caught the killer? Unless it was himself? Schizophrenic? In some black amnesiac moment of evil.

He could hear Gloria whooping it up inside, trying to regenerate the party atmosphere. What would happen to her – another of his lovers. Would she join the list of Angela, Joan and Fiona Strang if he and she stayed together? Mind you, Gloria would fight like a tigress, a woman possessed. She certainly loved life, had a real appetite for it.

But for her sake he couldn't risk it. Whereas if she was separated from him, she wouldn't be a target, no longer a link in that terrifying chain of death that led back to him.

Besides, all that talk, innuendo, scorn, mockery over months and months had taken its toll on him. He'd been called more names than he'd have thought possible: toy-boy, male prostitute, Casanova, were just some of the cleaner ones. He couldn't take it any more.

He was twenty-eight and what had started out as a charming, fun, relaxation had been made to seem dirty, almost perverted.

16

He'd better stick to younger women in future: that way they'd all probably live longer and he'd regain his self-respect. He hated the picture of him as some sort of prostitute, selling his body to rich middle-aged women in return for money and gifts. It just hadn't been like that but no one would believe him. He'd become like some walking dirty seaside post card, a figure of fun, a degenerate phallic symbol.

Gloria swayed out to greet him, flourishing a brandy bottle. "Old sour puss has gone I see. Good riddance, gate-crashing your welcome home party like that, trying to put the mockers on and spoil everything. Well we won't let him, will we?"

She gave Karl a smacking kiss full on the mouth. "I've got a bottle here. What say we sneak off away from the others, find a quiet corner and get to know this bottle pretty well. Then, who knows, I might let you take advantage of me."

"Terrific," Karl hastily agreed and steered her away round the side of the bungalow to the gazebo.

"Gloria. I have something to say to you. This trial has made me do a lot of thinking, mainly about us."

"I know, I know." Gloria eagerly gabbled, interjecting. "I've thought the same thing myself. We've lost too much time, haven't we? All those months with you locked away on remand." She was in danger of becoming maudlin. "God how I wanted you sometimes." Her eyes became fierce, predatory. "I've felt I could break down the walls to get to you, feel your body on mine. Anyway we've a lot of lost time to make up for. Why not here?" And she looked around for a dry, comfortable spot to lie down upon.

Karl restrained her with a firm, sharp grip. "No Gloria, it's not that at all. Of course I wanted you too but that's all got to be in the past. We have to end this now before we are in too deep again. Stick with me and you'll be killed like the others."

Gloria was watching his eyes trying to make out what he was saying, her temper fluctuating wildly.

'Stop, stop a minute will you? I can't follow all this. You say you want me like I want you, but then you say we have to finish for the good of my health? Well I'm not afraid, so why should you be?" Her hand was on her hip and working feverishly on her beaded sash.

"Gloria, I'm going to save your life, whether you want me to

17

or not. I couldn't have another death on my conscience. What if I did these killings myself without knowing it? In future you should steer well clear of me."

Gloria snarled: "So all this is for my benefit? Did I ask you to quit? Did I ask you to save me? I can look after myself buddy. Any man would have to move pretty damn fast to get me. I'd see him off first with anything that was handy." And she pulled up a wicked looking wooden stake from the flower bed.

"I'd stab him with this, like a pig. No, cut the crap. Behind all these fancy explanations you want out. You've had enough. Got your eye on another piece of skirt, have you? Well I won't give up, do you hear? I've stuck with you all through this trial and before, borne the insults and the jeers. Well I want my reward. I want you, and by God I'm going to have you. Try and leave me and you'll regret it."

"Gloria," Karl appealed to her.

"Get back, you ungrateful bastard." She weaved forward, poking at him with the sharp end of the stake. "I'll poke your eye out, tear your heart to shreds, I'll . . ."

Karl sidestepped and grabbed the stake out of her hands. With one quick movement he snapped it across his knee and threw the broken fragments into the flower bed. "Oh no you won't, you drunken old cow. Now be told: it's over." And he stormed away.

"Karl," she called after him, for the first time in a plaintive voice. "Karl . . . I'll kill myself if you go."

But he had disappeared around the side of the bungalow and could no longer hear her.

Karl swept into the living-room and immediately fell in with Judy and Sarah.

Judy grinned at him and took his arm. "Hey, wipe away that frown. You're supposed to be celebrating. Who's made you glum. Not Gloria?"

Seething, Karl admitted as much. "Look," he said urgently, "can we get out of here? It's giving me the creeps and any minute Gloria may be after my hide with a cleaver."

"Glad to see the spark and humour returning to Karl," Judy said to Sarah, "what do you think?"

"What are we waiting for?" was the reply, and Sarah gave Karl's other arm an affectionate tug. "Right then, let's escape the wicked witch of the north, a quick exit, goodbyes not advisable I think."

Judy led the way outside to her bright red Ferrari parked in the drive. They all clambered in, and then leaving the half-hearted party behind, sped down the lane.

Groups of villagers were morosely lingering on corners or walking down from the outlying farms. Worryingly, they had clubs and other home-made weapons in their hands.

As the car slowed for a bend the figures began to move faster, converging on the car. "Hold on folks!" Judy cried and accelerated out of the bend.

Now there was a banshee call going up from the crowd that was forming on either side of the village main street.

"Murderer!"

"Lady killer!"

"Swine!"

Fists were waved and grasping arms tried to grab the Ferrari's bodywork and slow the car down.

"Watch out," Karl yelled as Judy seemed about to mow down a large, aggressive farmer.

But in the battle of wills he lumbered out of the way just in time, with surprising agility. "Maniac!" the farmer called after the car.

One heavy booted foot managed to collide with the driver side door. "The clod's dented the bodywork I'm sure." Judy snarled.

Eyes gleaming and fixed on the long incline ahead, she changed gear and the car roared out of the village.

The huge boulders hung threatening as the car began to pull up, threading its way round the twists and turns in the road.

"This would be the place." Karl muttered. "If they take us now, God help us."

Judy nodded but her face was determined, hard, implacable.

Sarah kept searching the landscape for hidden figures. then shouted, "Look out!"

Two youths in battered corduroys and jerkins were levering a boulder using a plank, high up on the left. There was a crack, and a lurch, and then the boulder was spinning down with a sound like distant thunder.

"Oh no," Sarah let out. "Hurry, if you don't want us all killed."

Karl and Sarah clung to the sides of the car, as Judy put her foot on the pedal down to the floor. The gears screamed and the

19

car yanked itself forward shuddering and shaking with the exertion.

The boulder was bouncing now, an uncontrollable force. They could see the grey pitted marks on it like the craters on the moon. It seemed to launch itself into the air like a giant projectile and crashed into the road only yards ahead of them.

Shards of stone splintered off hitting the fender and windscreen, and then the boulder was careering on its way again down the hillside. A cheer went up from the youths above followed by curses when they saw how near the miss had been.

"We'll get you Lawrence, and your fancy pieces. Don't you ever dare to come back."

Judy relaxed her foot off the pedal a fraction and the car stopped jerking and protesting. "Well that was close. Nice friends you've got."

"They're no friends of mine. It's unbelievable how people can turn on you. Did you see the hatred in their eyes?"

"Well you'd better believe it, if you're ever thinking of coming back here again."

Karl looked back down the incline, towards the stone farms and cottages with their decaying outhouses, grazing pastures and one main street. "Me come back here? You must be joking. Never wouldn't be too long."

"Not even for Gloria?"

"Your mother never wants to see me again. She made that very clear."

"And you?"

'Me? I'm well out of it."

'That's just what I wanted to hear." And exhilarated Judy took the corner over the crest of the last hill and down the other side.

Sarah looked questioningly at Judy and then withdrew into herself again. She'd just have to watch and wait like always. You could never tell with Judy.

Chapter Four

Half an hour later the Ferrari pulled up outside Judy and Sarah's town flat.

The block was in a corner plot just opposite a major roundabout and near an up-market arcade with restaurants, wine bars and dress shops.

Judy, a spring in her step, led the way up to the flat and let them all in. There was a spacious lounge with art deco prints on the walls and filled with reproduction furniture, decorative if not particularly comfortable. The exception was a large flower upholstered chair like a giant petal, which Sarah took possession of by curling up in it.

Karl was taken by Judy on a little tour culminating in her bedroom. Without preliminaries she pulled him inside the door and kissed him passionately.

"Remember which bedroom to head for in the dark," she whispered and then bounced out again into the kitchenette.

"Coffee everyone?"

"Yes please," Karl and Sarah chorused and then laughed, with slight embarrassment.

Sarah's warm, attentive gaze followed Karl round as he looked at the pictures and then stared out of the window at the leafy common to the rear of the flats.

"You're pretty well fixed here, aren't you?"

Sarah nodded. "It suits us well. Judy needs access to the centre of town to do her interior design, as you can see," and Sarah indicated the room as Judy's handiwork, "and I can reach the nurseries by a ten minute walk." She smiled at him: "Horticulture not babies. Yet."

"Here we are, you two," said Judy breaking up their cosy confidences, and she handed round the coffee mugs.

"To your freedom," she toasted Karl.

As she sat down on a slim white chair with a narrow back, Judy added, "Mother was far too old for you. We tried to hint but you were . . . preoccupied."

"I'd rather not discuss Gloria if you don't mind."

Judy exchanged glances with Sarah. "OK."

Sarah sipped her coffee and nodded.

"You can stay here with us – can't he Sarah? – till you find your feet again."

Sarah acquiesced, but inside she was confused. Like Judy she was attracted to Karl with his moody good looks. However she also resented the intrusion, disturbing the mysterious intimacy of her life with Judy.

"Well that's settled then," Judy went gaily on. "Two women here with you after all that male company on remand. It must be quite a shock for you."

Karl detected a sort of malicious pleasure and probing at his feelings. "Yes, I missed women's company."

"The ultimate ladies' man, that's how you're painted."

"But there's much more to Karl than that," Sarah intervened.

Judy turned on Sarah sharply. "Of course there is, I know that. Haven't you things to do sister dear?"

"Not a thing," Sarah smiled back her sweetest smile, and settled down further into the petal fabric of the chair.

"You're musical, I hear?" Sarah asked Karl.

"That's a matter of opinion," Karl laughed modestly. "But I do play sax and a bit of trumpet. Acid house jazz."

"How riveting," Judy put in.

But Sarah and Karl ignored her.

"And before that? I have to tell you there are all sorts of rumours about why you returned from London."

"All true," Karl laughed again. "I was doing some photographic work. Even took a revealing one of royalty which ended up in a German magazine."

"So you were one of those paparazzi?" Judy sneered.

"Sort of. But it's cut throat and, well, there can be blackmail as well. I wouldn't go in for it and left. That's all there is to it."

"Fascinating," and Judy beamed at Karl. "I knew there was

something interesting about you. All this local handyman stuff was never you. I could tell that."

"Oh you could?"

"Yes," Judy breathed. "I'm artistic too. Maybe we could work together sometime?"

Sarah gave here a warning shake of the head but Judy chose to ignore her.

Karl finished his coffee. "Sounds good. I'm tired of fixing leaking roofs and dripping taps."

"I'm sure you are. There must be other things you can do better."

Sarah raised her eyes to the ceiling and took this as her cue to leave. "If anyone wants me – which seems unlikely – I'll be in my greenhouse, with my orchids."

"Don't go," Karl urged her, but a look from Judy told her not to linger.

"That's all right, I'll see you later – for supper."

Sarah was as good as her word and Judy relished having Karl to herself for several hours. Then the door chimes rang.

"Who's that?" Judy angrily stalked to the door. Wrenching it open she snapped, "Yes?"

An undersized rotund young man in an orange pullover and with short, spiked hair bobbed on the threshold. Striking pop-eyes stared back at her – then past her. "Karl!" he whooped.

At the voice Karl jumped up with fond delight. "Bug-eyes, where did you spring from?"

"Don't mind me," said Judy stepping aside as the young man catapulted himself into the living-room. He and Karl slapped each other on the back heartily.

Then Karl looked over his half-brother's shoulder to Judy. "Judy, you remember Gary?"

Reluctantly Judy acknowledged a faint recollection.

Suddenly Gary drew hack, sheepish. "I'm really sorry to have missed you at your welcome home party. I only found out about it at the last minute and by the time I got there you'd left with Judy and Sarah."

Karl suspected that Gary had been deliberately left off the party list and was both sorry and angry. People were always hurting Gary for no good reason and he only came back for more. "Forget it," Karl reassured him. "You must have a drink with me

23

to celebrate."

"I'll put some coffee on then shall I?" Judy sulked towards the kitchenette.

"Coffee for my better half? Never. Surely you've something stronger?"

Reluctantly Judy found some scotch and poured two smallish measures. The last thing she wanted was these two getting legless together and Gary crashing out there. She had other plans for Karl later.

"Cheers. Here's to my favourite bug-eyed monster."

Judy thought she heard an insult, but she was wrong.

Gary grinned from ear to ear. "Cheers, you remembered."

How could Karl forget? From childhood Gary had loved science fiction comics, acting out the monsters as his party piece.

"Go on, it's been so long," Karl encouraged him.

Gary became bashful. "I couldn't, not in front of company, cold."

"Here, this'll warm you up then," and Karl grabbed the whisky bottle and to Judy's consternation sloshed a generous measure into Gary's glass.

Gary downed it and began to glow inside. He banged down his glass and then seemed to swell, arms and legs extended, while an imaginary shell seemed to grow on his back. Then he capered about, waving imaginary antennae and emitting strange buzz noises and ethereal cries.

Karl joined in, alternatively chasing him and escaping his clutches, till they both grabbed each other and collapsed in a hilarious, sozzled heap on the carpet.

Karl wiped his eyes. "It seems ages since we've had fun like that."

"Yes, without you I never do it."

Thank goodness for that, thought Judy, and retreated to her bedroom for a lie down.

Karl and Gary picked themselves up, refilled their drinks, and began to reminisce about the old days; about the children's home, the mother they barely knew and their two fathers.

"I heard Frank died," Gary took up.

"Yes, just out of prison would you believe. Todd came and saw me after it had been in the newspapers. I told him then I wasn't going to the funeral."

"Why not?"

"After the way he treated me, his only son? Ditching me in that home. I never saw him for months. Then he dragged me round London after him."

"Sounds rotten."

"It was. He was totally out of it by the end. Had all sorts of mad delusions about one final big job. A robbery."

Gary nodded, and then the turn of the conversation seemed to have sobered him up. "I'm really sorry Karl. Anyway, you and me won't lose touch, will we?" He hesitated. "Todd told me to pass on his regards."

"Him! You shouldn't let Todd use you Gary. He's bad news."

Gary squirmed. "I know. But he gets me things."

"Not steroids again?"

Gary nodded. "I'm body-building. Look." He beamed proudly.

"You bloody idiot. Steroids will kill you."

"Please don't shout at me. What shall I tell Todd?"

Karl was tempted, but settled for a non-committal, "Tell him I'll be in touch. Now – " he nodded towards Judy's bedroom – "I'm going to be tied up."

Gary's eyes opened up more than usual. "Lucky you."

They both burst out laughing and Karl slapped Gary on the back as he led him to the front door. "Hey, that was pretty good coming from you. Maybe you're sharpening up after all. Take care, and watch out for Todd."

Gary smiled. "It's been good to see you. I knew they couldn't find you guilty, not a pal, a brother like you."

Gary let himself out of the door and Karl returned to the lounge. Judy re-emerged from the bedroom. "Has he gone?"

Karl nodded, but added, "Don't give me a hard time over Gary. He's my half-brother and I love him, so no cracks."

"Did I say a word?"

"No but . . ."

"I've other things on my mind now."

"Like what?"

"I'll show you."

And slowly she unbuttoned Karl's shirt and peeled it off. Next she helped him kick off his shoes and socks, and reached for the belt of his trousers.

Playfully he halted her hands. "Just a minute, this is rather one

25

sided," and he reached for the zip on her dress.

As the dress hung caught at her waist, Judy clung to Karl and they kissed passionately and they stumbled onto the floor.

Judy pressed Karl's head back. "Much more comfortable through there," and she indicated her bedroom. Karl nodded and they finished undressing in there.

Then all the pent up hunger of months on remand was released, and Judy felt as if she were being eaten alive.

Her long white arms and legs entwined about him and her blood red nails raked his shoulders.

Karl, back to the bedroom door, vaguely sensed another presence. "Come and join us," Judy lazily invited.

Karl slowly lifted himself and squinted towards the doorway. Sarah was standing framed there, naked, hesitant.

"What's all this?" Karl wondered.

"Sarah and I share everything, including men. It's a principle with us, take it or leave it."

Karl was past caring. "Sounds pretty kinky, but I'll take it."

Sarah walked slowly and purposefully forward and lifted the covers on the nearside of the bed. She slipped inside and insinuated herself into Karl's arms.

"Some crazy homecoming," Karl muttered and then kissed her.

Chapter Five

Karl paused outside Harold Todd's surgery. He was there reluctantly, since Todd gave him the creeps, but he didn't want to make Gary suffer at Todd's hands by refusing. The surgery was part way down a terraced block in an unfashionable part of the town. Karl looked casually at the gold plaque, and then looked again: it wasn't the same as before. No longer did it bear the title 'Doctor Todd'; now the word inscribed was 'Therapist'. What on earth did that mean? Karl wondered as he went inside.

There was no reception desk and Karl proceeded straight through to Todd's consulting room. He knocked.

"Come."

Hackles rising already, Karl entered.

Todd was seated behind his desk. Involuntarily Karl shuddered before the bloated figure with his big, potato head and long, flattened ears. Todd had small, grey eyes and was bald apart from some little tufts which sprouted on either side of his head. He had a long, fat torso and short stumpy legs.

"At last. You took your time. Didn't Gary tell you it was urgent?" Todd spoke quickly as if his tongue was too big for his mouth.

"I'm here aren't I? That should be good enough. Or I can leave right now."

"Now don't get mad," Todd made an effort to be amiable. "Sit down. You've had a bad time. Congratulations . . . is that the right word?"

"I don't know, you're the one with the education. By the way, why the change of plaque. What happened to 'Doctor Todd'?"

"I was struck off," Todd muttered distastefully. "Not one of the

BMA would speak up for me. Not one. Just because I fell foul of the law."

Karl thought all this affronted dignity was a bit rich coming from Todd, whose medical practice was notorious. "So you're a Therapist now?"

Todd nodded gloomily. "They can't stop me being that," he said with grim satisfaction.

"Well what do you want to see me about?" Karl was becoming restive.

Todd paused. "Sad about your father."

Karl blinked. "There was nothing sad about it. He was better off dead. He was no use to anybody, not after all the prison he'd done."

"Harsh words," remonstrated Todd. "Frank wasn't all bad. In fact he had some excellent qualities."

"Name one."

"Well he was what you would call a man's man."

"He was bonkers. Always on about one last big job, right up to the end."

Todd winked at him, his heavy jowl wobbling. "He left a fortune, hidden somewhere."

"Are you touched?"

"Certainly not. Don't play the innocent. Where is it?"

Karl looked him straight in the eye. "This is fantastic. There is no hidden fortune. It must be one of those yarns my father was always spinning. You should know that."

Todd wouldn't be moved. "Not this time. I was in on those jobs. None of that bullion was recovered."

"Well, I know nothing about it."

"You would say that, wouldn't you? You aren't keeping it all for yourself by any chance?"

"That's ridiculous!"

"Is it? I hear you've offered a fortune to Randle to find the killer."

Karl was astounded. "How did you learn about that?"

"Easy. Now ask me a hard one like: who was the killer? Oh yes, I know."

Karl shook his head. Then disbelief was followed by anger, horror. "Tell me," Karl threatened ominously.

"Don't be stupid. I only trade information. You tell me where the fortune is and maybe . . ."

"Trade!" Karl almost screamed. "When I was nearly sent down for murder?"

"You were my patient, remember. You were so out of your head, you were capable of anything."

"I ought to kill you for saying that. You disgust me."

"Then you'd never know one way or the other."

Saliva seemed to fill Karl's mouth. "I'm sick of all this talk. It's crazy, and I don't believe a word of it."

"You will. Go away and think about it. You'll see it makes sense. I never over-play my hand. Ask anybody."

Karl rose and petulantly kicking over his chair, stormed out.

Lazily Todd watched Karl go. Impulsive young man, unsettled, could jump either way. Then Todd's expression hardened. All those youthful good looks wasted on that playboy. What had he ever done? Strictly small time, with his whisky still, and his acid house parties. Selling out of a suit case on the Birdham Road; now that really was the pits.

And to think that his father Frank was a famous bank robber. With all that bullion stashed away somewhere. He'd have confided in his only son: must have.

But Karl was so difficult, so prickly – and could be dangerous. What was that old nick name? Snake eyes.

Then intolerable envy took hold of Todd. Karl had everything – casual good looks, the cool, that women went for.

Angrily, Todd pulled himself together and shouted out to the back.

Seconds later Gary sheepishly came through.

"You heard?"

Gary nodded.

"I want that fortune. I'm entitled. Karl knows where it is."

"I don't think he does. He's never said anything."

"You're not paid to think. Leave that to me. I'm equipped for it, you're not. Now, I want to find out what Karl knows."

"He wouldn't tell me now, even if he did know."

"You can pry, can't you? What about these two sisters he's shacked up with now. Make yourself useful there, keep you ear to the door, you may learn something that way."

Gary's head went down and he sulked. "It's not fair. I get all the dirty jobs. I won't do it."

Todd rubbed his fleshy hands together. "You want the steroids don't you? A new batch just came in."

Gary wavered.

"Think of the women Karl's got. You could have them too."

Gary's popping eyes lit up with naïve hope. "You really think so?"

"No doubt about it. Women love a hunk of a man."

"Well OK, I'll see what I can do," Gary mumbled.

"I didn't quite catch that."

"Yes." Gary flared up, then fell silent, brooding. He couldn't betray Karl.

He'd have to tell Karl everything. Karl would figure a way out. He always did. Karl was his hero.

Chapter Six

Back at the flat Karl poured out his heart to Judy: "Todd claimed to know who the killer was. But would he warn me? Not unless I told him the whereabouts of a fortune my father is supposed to have left hidden. It sickened me."

Judy's mind was working overtime, calculating if there was real money to be had from her young lover. "And there's no fortune?" she began hesitantly.

"Not you too? None that I know of. I suppose it's possible. Dad was always full of mad schemes, and buried treasure would have appealed to him."

"So what are you going to do?"

Karl was gnawing his nail, concentrating. "I don't know. Maybe bluff Todd, but he'll only try the same with me. Which leaves us nowhere."

"Have you any idea where your father might have buried a fortune?"

Karl threw up his hands. "It could be any of a dozen places. Though I suppose he might have chosen his old hideout in the village."

Just then the door-bell rang and Judy admitted Gary who as before burst in eager to tell Karl all.

When Gary had spilled all Todd's plans and instructions, Karl went moody and disappeared into a corner to think.

But when he re-emerged there was a savage grin on his face. "Thanks a million, Gary. What do you say to leading Todd on a wild goose chase? Judy?"

"Just try and stop me." Excitement was right in her line.

"Good. Gary, you split back to Todd and tell him he's panicked us into action. If I know Todd he'll follow."

"Right big brother. This should be something to see, eh?"
"You bet."

Gary grinned back and hastened out on his mission.

"Can you trust Gary to get it right?" Judy was sceptical.

Karl eyed her coldly. "Don't ever put him down. He's family and he'll do anything for me."

"I don't doubt it. But is he competent?"

"We'll soon find out won't we? Or are you chickening out?"

"You know I'm not."

"Well let's go – in your Ferrari."

"I thought so. Oh, all right."

They hurtled round the town for a time flagrantly advertising their presence till Karl was certain they had picked up a tail. Then they were off up into the hills.

They sped along river gorges, by huge willow trees and sparkling brooks. They roared up steep inclines into bare tops where the surface was a burnished brown and even sheep were scarce. Then down again screeching round hairpin bends, marked by white boulders, and skirting farms with their long muddied tracks and the yapping of dogs on chains.

By a ford in the river Karl yelled, "Quick, out of the car. The rest is on foot."

Bewildered, Judy jumped out after him. "I hope you know where you're going?" Already her thigh length black boots were muddy.

"Of course I do. Give me your hand," and he helped her clamber over the huge stones which bridged the ford for walkers.

Hand in hand they spirited up the track into the woods, as the Land-rover which had been chasing them hove into sight.

Scrambling over the ridge at the top, Karl looked back to see Todd and his cronies leaping out and rushing past the Ferrari in pursuit.

Judy's red cashmere jacket with gold buttons was caught on a bush and they lost precious minutes releasing it. But then Karl knew where to make a diversion along an unexpected path, disturbing squirrels and a fox on the way.

Judy brushed an overhanging cobweb from her face, and then saw a clearing. "Are we there yet?" she panted and then added, "I mean, we are headed for somewhere. We're not just blundering about?"

Karl grinned at her with his superior knowledge of the landscape. "You don't have much faith do you? Not far. Look."

Judy followed his finger and saw some caves in the hillside opposite. Heartened she followed him, clambering over dead tree trunks and pitching headlong as her foot caught in a rabbit hole. "Damn!"

Karl helped her up and laughed at her muddy state.

"It's no laughing matter, you bloody imbecile." She stared down at her mud-spattered jacket and elegant black cord trousers. Then she laughed too. "My God, what a sight I look. Oh well, never mind. On we go."

Admiring her spirit Karl led her up the final incline to the caves. He paused, watched and listened but was confident that they had lost their pursuers a long way back.

Judy let out a gasp: she'd found his cave. "What have you done?" She was amazed.

"Oh, a few home comforts."

There was an iron bedstead and mattress, a couple of small chipped cabinets, a whole pile of electrical equipment, some plastic garden chairs, and to the side an arrangement of barrels, tubes, demijohns and glasses.

"That's my whisky still. I'll let you try some later if you like."

Judy was dubious but let it pass whilst rummaging around. "What's this?"

Karl barred the way to a little cave which ran off the main one. "Out of bounds. I'll perhaps show you later – if we're both in the mood."

Judy raised a cynical eyebrow, moved back and began cleaning herself up.

"You'll find some water in that urn. And there's towels and maybe some clothes in that trunk there. Have a scout around."

While Judy followed his advice Karl disappeared and returned with two glasses of wine. "Where's this come from?" Judy eyed it suspiciously.

"Would you believe, the local supermarket?"

Judy laughed and they drank a toast to their success in evading their pursuers. One toast led to others and soon they were playfully chasing each other for the bottle. Collapsing onto the bed, they began kissing and fondling each other, finally dragging off each other's clothes.

They made love with the smell of briar and blackberries in their nostrils and their mouths soaked in red wine.

Afterwards Karl flicked a switch on his cassette recorder and the sound of him playing his sax filled the cave. The sound began slowly, ethereal, and then became more sensual gradually growing in volume. Quietly Karl disappeared to the side cave and then minutes later returned.

Judy was ready to make love again, but instead Karl dragged her by the hand into the side cave.

There her eyes widened in shock and disbelief. On ledges all around shone candles like a fairy grotto and in the centre was a pagan altar with a statue upon it, swathed in vine leaves.

"What's that?" croaked Judy.

"Dionysus, the ancient god. He's a bit battered, but I couldn't believe it when I dug him up. Think of all the ceremonies he's witnessed. Come close, he won't bite."

Judy and Karl approached the statue. At first Judy was intoxicated with the macabre, exotic atmosphere. Gracefully she danced for a moment. Then the gloom began to seep into her and she shivered in revulsion.

"Let me out of here. It's horrible. I've read about black magic sacrifices. Don't kill me."

Karl was shocked. "Kill you? This isn't black magic. It's the cult of Dionysus. The life giver."

"Well whatever it is, I don't know what you get up to here, but I'm a town girl."

Spooked, she stumbled back up to the other cave and grabbed her clothes. "And turn that bloody screeching music off."

Quietly, Karl did as she asked, and put on his own clothes. Then he took her in his arms again. "There's really nothing to be frightened of."

Judy was defiant, angry at being accused of fear. "I know that," she snapped. "Let's get out of here, it's like a junk yard."

Karl sighed and led the way back down to the car.

Judy was still seething as she re-entered the flat. Karl caught the front door as it swung back upon him.

"Hey," he protested.

"Are you still here?" Judy called back from over her shoulder as she headed for the bathroom. "Close the door behind you on the way out."

"I'm not going anywhere." Karl slammed the door shut and stood his ground.

Judy whirled round. "Oh yes you are. I've had enough of your antics. Dragging me out into the middle of nowhere, into some smelly cave and as for that corny shrine . . ."

"You didn't seem to mind when we made love. And that shrine is truly ancient, and could heal you."

"Heal me?" Judy poked herself in the chest, incredulous. "So now I'm the one who's mad."

Karl's brow became furrowed with annoyance. "Who's said anything about mad? But there's a very strange atmosphere here with you two, and that three in a bed routine."

Judy's eyes blazed as she tore off her besmirched red jacket. "You weren't complaining as I recall. Are you turning prudish all of a sudden? That's odd from a man who likes dancing naked around pagan statues."

Quietly Karl told her: "You did that remember. Not me. I never told you to do that."

Judy was caught off balance and threw her jacket on to the sofa in a scrunched up ball. "Well anyway, I don't know why a good looking bloke like you gets mixed up in all that weirdness."

Karl sat down. "It's just a way of reaching a state, ecstasy."

"Oh yes, 'ecstasy' – we know all about that. Todd can always come up with a supply of pills. Can't he Sarah?"

Karl looked around to see Sarah emerging from her bedroom. She wore a long Laura Ashley floral smock and sandals. Her hair was tied back. "Sorry, I couldn't help overhearing."

"Well what do you think of Karl dragging me up to his cave?"

Sarah leant across and put her arm on Judy's. "I don't see the harm."

Judy pushed Sarah away. "Are you siding with Karl? Well you have him. I can't stomach all this phoney spirituality. I'm off to have a bath."

Sarah and Karl sat on looking at each other. "I've never seen Judy so shocked before," confided Sarah.

"I didn't mean to frighten her."

Sarah touched Karl with her long sensitive fingers. "I don't see any demons in you."

"What about skeletons in the closet?"

Sarah frowned and placed a finger over his lips. "Enough. Don't spoil everything." She took his face in her hands and kissed him.

Then drawing back she said, "You must show me your cave sometime – caveman." She grinned, patting his chest.

"Well this is a new side to you."

She smiled. "Oh I'm full of surprises. Judy isn't the only one. I can be dangerous too."

Chapter Seven

The ringing of the phone broke in on Karl and Sarah's intimacy. Sarah answered it and then screwed up her face as she passed the receiver to Karl: "It's Gloria for you. She sounds in a hell of a state."

Curious, Karl took the receiver. "Yes Gloria."

"Ah, there you are, you ratfink. Running off was bad enough but with my own daughters."

"Gloria please, it was for your own good as well as mine. Our affair had run its course. And the bottom line was I wouldn't see you on that death list. I really do care about you."

A snarl came down the phone. "From a safe distance, shacked up with those two tarts."

"Gloria stop that, don't talk about your own daughters like that."

"You ask them, I dare you." Then her tone changed into something hard, commanding: "Come up here now or you'll be sorry."

"I'm sorry now taking this call. Can't you get it in your head it's over."

"It's never over, not with me, unless I say so. I don't say so."

"Gloria be reasonable. Besides those vigilantes up there warned me off ever re-entering the village. They'd skin me alive."

"I'll do that and more if you don't come. I mean it Karl, I'm not messing, you come or you'll regret it for the rest of your life."

Karl racked his brains. Was she bluffing, or had she something on him, some damaging secret, perhaps to do with the murders? He had to find out.

Reluctantly he came on the line again: "All right Gloria, you win. I'll come up there – just to talk. But I can't see the point."

"You will!" And she rang off.

Sarah was aghast when Karl confirmed where he was going. "It's her old trick of emotional blackmail. She used it for years on Judy and I till we became wise to her. Take care, Gloria can be a proper handful when she gets going."

"I will." Glancing towards Judy's shut bedroom door he added, "In the circumstances I think I'd better take the bus."

Sarah nodded. "I think you had."

He kissed her and left. The bus wound slowly through the country lanes to the village. Karl alighted by the pub at the far end of the High Street and glanced from side to side. A couple of farmers were wandering down for a pint but no one seemed to be taking any notice of him.

He worked his way up the High Street, preparing himself at any moment to be accosted, but he emerged unscathed at the top and turned up the slight incline to Gloria's bungalow. All the lights were on and the sound of music filtered through the curtains.

Party for one, Karl thought as he rang the front door bell. There was no answer. He tried again with the same result. Then he pushed the door itself and it swung open. Karl was beginning to feel the whole thing was stage managed and he resented it. Serve Gloria right if he turned round and went out again.

But instead he progressed through the vestibule, calling out, "Gloria, Gloria," each time more impatiently.

He entered the lounge – and saw the noose gently swaying as it hung from the roof beam. A chair lay on its side, vacant below it.

"Bloody hell," he shouted, relieved that at least the noose was empty but angry at the melodramatics. She'd deliberately set it up, leaving the front door open so that the noose would be the first thing he encountered.

"Gloria, where are you, you wicked old bitch? I want a word with you."

He seethed, moving from room to room ready to vent his anger and contempt upon her. But she was nowhere to be found. He couldn't figure it out: surely she'd want to be close enough to see his reaction, savour his discomfort. Where was the joke when the audience had disappeared?

He searched through the bedrooms, even looking under the beds and behind the furniture, in case she was playing some elaborate game of hide and seek. He'd give her a piece of his mind when he found her, frightening the life out of him like this.

The back door was ajar and he stumbled out into the garden. Along there they'd said angry farewells at the party.

He turned to the left by the small garden shed and found her, lying sprawled on the earth, spluttering and choking. Karl bent down to nurse her and saw the ugly purple mark on her throat. So she'd tried to hang herself after all. But what was she doing out here in the garden?

He lifted her and carried her inside, carefully avoiding the lounge with its terrifying noose, and deposited her on her bed.

She lay there gasping, her eyes far away, whites showing, then gradually she came back to him. "Where am I?"

"I found you in the garden, and carried you here."

Gloria rubbed her throat. "Did you sneak up on me from behind and try to kill me?"

"Hey, hang on, you've got this all wrong. Remember the noose? I came in to find it. What happened?"

Gloria's head went down. "All right, I admit it. I wanted you to catch me in the act."

"Oh my God."

"I know it was a terrible thing to do but I was desperate. But when I stood on the chair and placed my head in the noose, someone from behind tried to knock the chair away."

"What?"

"I fought with my legs to keep the chair upright and kicked around at whoever it was. I was being strangled. It was awful, I thought I was dying."

"Gloria!"

"The noose must have slipped because somehow I prised my head free. Just in time, because the chair toppled over. I dragged myself out into the garden for air but he must have followed, and tried to strangle me there. I must have blacked out."

"Who was it?"

"I couldn't see. He crept up behind me."

Karl grabbed her and held her tight, kissing her cheeks. "I knew this would happen. The murderer would have you on his

39

list. That's why we must part now for ever, a clean break."

Gloria sagged back, jaw dropping. "How can you be so callous, just when I need you. Someone tries to kill me and you're going to walk away and leave me unprotected. What kind of man are you?"

"Not the kind who can play lover and bodyguard over you for the rest of your life. That stunt only backfired."

Gloria sat back, upright against the pillow. There were black patches under her eyes, and a dreadful purple mark around her neck.

"So that's it, the sum total of you and me. Nothing."

"Gloria stop all that. I'll ring the police. They'll give you the protection you need."

Gloria shook her head violently. "No police. They'd never understand."

"Gloria, that killer tried again tonight. You could have been murder victim number four."

"But I wasn't. What could I tell them? I never saw him – only you. They'd suspect you."

"But . . ."

"Forget it. It's no use."

"I wish I could. You're bad news."

"I know. Now come to bed, just for tonight. You can't refuse me that."

Karl looked down at her in self-disgust. Rent a body. Any woman had only to ask for the use of him and he obliged like a trained seal. They knew who was using who.

Once in bed Gloria clung to him possessively, keeping him from sleep. But the next thing he knew, hands were roughly shaking him.

"What? What's the matter?"

"Get up." A big man in a patched sports jacket overlapping a huge beer gut was pulling at him. "And for God's sake put some clothes on. We don't find you as appealing as these women do."

Karl rubbed his eyes. The bed was surrounded by half a dozen men. The smell of beer pervaded the room and their eyes were lit up.

Then Gloria screamed: "Don't go with them Karl. Stay here with me."

The men guffawed and the big one said, "You can't hide

behind women's skirts now. This is men's work."

Half dressed, Karl was dragged from Gloria's clawing arms and with a smack she was thrown back across the bed.

Like an armoured column the group sped Karl through the bungalow back to the lounge.

"Now what have we here?" the big man grinned. "Strange shenanigans going on in this house. Were you planning to top Gloria later like the rest?"

"Don't be crazy." Karl struggled frantically against the imprisoning arms. "You've got it all wrong. I didn't put the noose there."

"Well who did then?"

Karl refused to name Gloria.

"Anyway it doesn't really matter. The noose merely saves us a job. Right, get him up on that chair."

Another of the group set the chair on its legs below the noose and Karl was forced up on to it.

The big man drew another chair alongside and slipped the noose over Karl's head, while the other man tied Karl's hands behind him with a belt.

"We believe in country justice," the big man explained. "And no clever lawyer is going to get you off this time. You'll prey on no more village women after this."

Karl's eyes darted about desperately. "But I didn't do it. I was acquitted. You've no proof against me."

"If it weren't for you those three women would be alive and walking today. They were all your fancy pieces."

"But I tell you it wasn't me. They probably had the same postman, the same milkman. Does that make them murderers too?"

At the back a quiet man said, "He has a point."

"Thank you," Karl's voice was breaking. "I loved them all – all right made love to them all. Why should I kill them?"

"It does seem he'd be killing the golden goose," the quiet man continued.

"Will you shut up agreeing with him," the big man protested, but the mob was wavering. The lynch mentality was seeping away as they began to sober up and realise the enormity of their actions.

The big man's brother laid a hand on his arm. "I think we've done enough for one night. We've put the frighteners on him, that's sufficient. He won't come back here in a hurry."

The big man turned as he was led away by the others: "By God he'd better not come back. There'll be no reprieve next time. Now get your hands off me all of you. I still think we're making a mistake, letting him slip through our fingers."

The rest ushered him out and suddenly the bungalow was empty, as if they'd never been there.

Karl's head was swimming, and retaining his balance on the chair required acrobatic skill at that moment. He was totally alone with death, in that room. He had only to stumble and he'd be asphyxiated.

The horror made it hard for him to stay calm and keep his balance. It was so lonely up there, placed in a position of execution by his fellow man. And for what? Blind supposition without a shred of evidence.

Then Gloria appeared, and with her hand over her mouth immediately stifled a scream. Karl was glad because the reverberations might have upset his delicate balancing act.

He felt exposed, like an exhibit in a zoo, and utterly humiliated. With his head he tried to indicate the other chair.

Catching on, Gloria climbed up alongside him and released his head from the noose. Then she helped him down and released his hands.

They looked at each other with the cursed noose above them. He wanted to shout, abuse her for putting that dreadful thing up there which had nearly cost both their lives.

But he couldn't, he was too relieved. They held each other close. There was nothing left to say. Then Karl found the rest of his clothes and left.

Chapter Eight

Back at the sisters' flat Karl kept the awful events at Gloria's home locked inside himself. He was to blame for bringing all this down on Gloria and him. If only he had not been seduced into the role of toy boy, lover for rent by these women they'd all be alive now and he and Gloria would never have met: no hoax suicide, no attempted murder, no lynch mob.

Who was behind all this? Todd had said he knew who the murderer was. Could it be Todd himself? After all, he had been doctor to the victims. Or was there another man, in the shadows, envying Karl his success, wanting those particular women for himself and in despair killing them?

Another name was forcing itself forward, and resist as be might Karl had to face it. Gary, his half-brother. Gary knew all about Karl's love life, intimately, often calling at embarrassing moments. Gary had never had any success with women himself; could resentment have built up under the façade of playing the fool, only to erupt in murder? Had these steroids he was taking unbalanced his mind?

But Karl berated himself for thinking like this. Gary hero-worshipped him, would do anything for him, and was the kindest person he knew. It was impossible for Gary to kill anyone.

So where did that leave him? Waiting for a call from Randle he supposed, with some new evidence that might point in the right direction – even if it was towards himself. Randle had quit the police very suddenly after his acquittal. Should he read anything into that? His head was aching now.

Suddenly Judy marched in on his gloomy reflections and was a joy to see. Clearly stung at being upstaged by Sarah recently, she had decided to forgive Karl the cave incident. Secretly she was ashamed of bottling out of whatever orgiastic rites went on up there. She had an image of reckless abandon to maintain.

Today she was wearing a short red dress which showed off her long tanned legs. Her raven black hair was swept back in luscious profusion and she wore two looped gold earrings. Her green, almond shaped eyes had regained that excitement, that hint of danger which they had held at his welcome home party.

She was determined to regain the initiative, show him she was more than game for anything. Turning full circle in front of him, she said, "What do you think?"

Karl whistled. "You look fabulous."

"Thank you, kind sir."

She came to sit on his lap, planting a firm possessive kiss on his lips and moving her hand through his hair.

"A bit different than when I was covered from head to foot in mud."

Karl nodded. "Yes, I'm sorry about that. It was meant to be just a lark, leading Todd and his gang on a wild goose chase. It all got rather heavy at the end I'm afraid."

Pleased with herself for enticing an apology from him, Judy leant forward and nibbled his ear. Then she whispered – "Sometime you'll have to take me up there again and we'll see what spirits we can conjure up."

But Karl checked her with his hand. "No don't make light of it. It doesn't do to carelessly dabble in the occult."

"Don't tell me you believe all that nonsense?"

"I don't know, but there are strange forces at work we don't fully understand. That I do believe."

Judy was becoming impatient. "Well, whatever you say. But all this heavy reverence sounds rather boring, so let's leave it. I've much more exciting things in mind. Do you want to see me in action, earning my high salary?"

Politeness required Karl to agree. "Interior decorating?" It didn't sound very exciting to him.

Judy snorted with glee. "Of a sort. I'll just get my things." She went into her bedroom and returned with a large leather attaché case.

"Very professional," Karl commented.

Judy winked at him as she walked past and out of the door.

Rattled Karl hastened to catch up with her.

She drove him to a smart office block in the centre of town and together they took the lift to the top floor.

As she unlocked the office door, Judy explained: "It's good up here.We won't be disturbed."

Karl thought this a curious comment upon an interior design business but said nothing.

The office was furnished very casually with chairs and sofas, plenty of lights, and just one desk by the window.

Placing her case on the desk, Judy explained, "I've a client arriving in about five minutes. I need to change," – she indicated a clothes closet off the main office – "and you can wait in the inner office if you don't mind. Mustn't frighten him off first time round by appearing mob handed."

Karl thought the two of them hardly qualified as 'mob handed' but acquiesced and went through to the other room. Judy probably didn't want him hanging around, putting her off while she made her sales pitch to this client.

Accordingly he sat down on a swivel chair and inspected a couple of filing cabinets but they were empty. Time dragged and he wondered what Judy was doing in there but did not wish to annoy her by emerging again.

Finally he heard the office door open and a male voice enquired within. He heard Judy's voice very even and calm. They seemed to be discussing the client's requirements.

Then there followed a long silence interrupted by the occasional rustling, and clicking sounds.

Finally Judy's voice could be heard again very harsh and commanding. The man was complaining, angrily.

Karl jumped up and opened the door. A portly half-naked man was now pleading: "Don't tell my wife."

Judy, dressed in leather from head to toe with long thigh length boots, countered: "But she employed me."

"What?" the man spluttered in horror.

"Wives pay me to test their husbands. You've just failed."

"But we didn't do anything."

Judy smiled. "You would have." Then she grinned at Karl, "Come in, we've just finished. I've everything I need."

"Please!" the man was deeply embarrassed now, trying to cover himself up. Then angrily again: "Bitch. I'll get you for

45

this."

It all looked degrading to Karl. "What are you up to Judy?"

"I'll explain as we go. Must hurry now." She gathered up her belongings.

"You're not leaving him like this?"

"Of course. Come on, hurry up. You do catch on slowly sometimes." And she hurried Karl out with her.

Once down in the car, she laughed gaily. "It's not quite what you think – or the clients. They pay up front. I lead them on, but only far enough to convince their wives who retain me. Sometimes the men make a better counter offer, not to tell."

"That's despicable."

"That's business. They shouldn't be going in for that sort of thing."

"And why was I there?"

"Well that's the beauty of it. I need some muscle, because some of these men become aggressive and try to turn the tables, which is where you come in."

Karl gasped at her effrontery. "I'm not your pimp."

Judy's jaw went down, sulking. "Oh well, please yourself. But it seemed a marvellous idea. And you are living rent free in the flat."

As Karl looked away from her she coaxed him, "Oh, come on Karl, it's only a bit of a lark. These men and their wives can afford it. Stupid punters, and they get their money's worth – well their wives do."

"And what does that make them – and you?"

"Oh well, if you're going to be all moralistic about it, there's nothing more to be said."

"Oh yes there is," and Karl forced Judy to draw the car into the kerb and stop.

"You must give up all this. It's degrading, and dangerous."

"Must I, mister high and mighty. I barely know you, but here you are giving me orders. Well it won't wash."

"Judy, for my sake."

"You can talk. What about that illegal whisky still? How many other scams have you working?"

"Petty stuff, a bit of fun, to give the police the run around after what they did to my dad. But you, you've your whole life ahead of you, you're bright and beautiful, and you'll ruin it all."

Judy was abashed. No one had cared about her like that for as long as she could remember. "That's a bit strong isn't it? I can give it up any time I want to."

Karl clutched at the statement eagerly. "Then make it now. You and I, we don't need all this hassle. We can make a fresh start." Inspiration carried him away: "Marry me."

"Marry you?"

"Yes, put all this tawdry business behind us."

"But I hardly know you."

"What you see is what you get. As for you, you're the most beautiful, exciting, wonderful girl I've ever met. I can't bear to see you throw it all away."

"I have to decide now?"

Karl hesitated then went with what he felt. "Yes."

Judy calculated. A weak man would have given her time. She needed to forestall Sarah, never mind their old talk of share and share alike. Karl was handsome, with a wild, reckless streak like her own, and romantic.

"Very well." She kept him on tenterhooks for a moment: "Yes."

"Marvellous." Karl grabbed her and swung her round out of the car, dancing with her on the verge. "We'll be the happiest couple there's ever been. We'll do everything, go everywhere, not give a damn, live as we please."

Finally, an hour later, back at the flat, when she had calmed him down, Judy came and quietly sat beside him. "I want to tell you something to make you understand about me and Sarah, the way we are."

Judy took a deep breath then forced herself to continue: "We were at a party for local business men. I'm convinced Todd drugged Sarah and me. Because they raped us. We were so out of it we could do nothing to stop them."

Karl put his arms around her. "I'm so sorry."

But Judy did not collapse or soften. Instead she seemed to harden. "So we made a pact. To stick together through thick and thin. Let no man separate or hurt us. And look, I'm breaking it. But I can't help it. I love you."

"I know. I'll make everything all right, you'll see. We'll put all this horror behind us, I promise."

Judy grabbed his arm vehemently. "You will, won't you? You

won't let me down. If you did, I swear to God I'd kill you. I can't go through that kind of hell ever again. I just can't."

"Hey, hey," Karl soothed her. "You won't have to. Now where can we get some champagne? And Sarah – we must tell her. She must be the first to know."

Chapter Nine

Judy and Karl were up there, he knew. Randle waited by the shopping arcade, which gave him an excellent vantage point to observe the flats. How much longer, he wondered. He was determined to quiz them separately. His was a very subtle, devious ploy which required the utmost ingenuity and skill.

Despite himself he began picturing Karl and Judy together in the flat. Damn that good looking playboy. Given a straight choice she was bound to prefer Karl to a middle-aged, grizzled has been, as Randle knew people regarded him. Too many years on the force, too many sleepless stake-outs, too many rancid cups of coffee and undigested fast food meals were bound to make a man's face puffy and worn. What had he to show for it? One commendation but no promotion. So he'd turned it in. Why ruin his health further, when the villains like Karl walked away from their crimes and enjoyed the high life – the fancy flats, beautiful women, villas on the Costa del Sol.

Well he was going to have himself some of that, before it was too late. No longer would he play the patsy.

As for that fool Karl: if he wanted to pay Randle thousands of pounds up front accumulating more evidence against himself, then let him. Karl's money would supplement his police pension nicely. If only Karl had been convicted, life would be so much better, safer. Then he could have his pick of women with no Karl to shut him out. Revenge, that was something worth having.

Just then he saw Karl scurrying out of the street door to the flats. Maybe he was off on some errand.

Randle had better be quick.

He waited till Karl was out of sight then dodged the traffic on the roundabout to make a bee-line for the flats. Minutes later he was ringing the bell.

Subdued, Judy answered. She registered vague recognition. "Yes?"

"You remember me, Randle."

Judy cast her mind back. "The trial. You were the detective on the case." Then she really began to remember. "You came busting in on Karl's welcome home party. Goodbye." She tried to slam the door on him.

"Not so fast. I've a few questions to ask you."

"About what?"

"Let me in and you'll find out."

Judy slunk back, her green eyes downcast, suspicious. "All right, what do you want?"

Randle strolled about the flat, acclimatising himself, weighing up the money lavished on it.

Ignoring her question he asked his own. "Was it a good session in town? Profitable?"

"Pardon?"

"Did your client come through? After you and Karl piled out, a rather sad specimen who'd obviously too hurriedly dressed appeared. Completely dazed. He didn't seem to know if he was coming or going."

"I don't know what you are talking about." Judy stood. hands on hips, trying to bluff it out but her lips twitched nervously.

"Please, spare me. I've quite a dossier on you. Names, dates. – photographs. Weird little sessions, aren't they? The clients look so pathetic."

"I suppose you drool over it all you pervert."

'That's rich coming from you. Anyway, what wouldn't you give to know where that dossier is now?"

Judy paced: she'd changed back into her short red dress, an angry flame passing to and fro before his eyes.

"Well?" Her eyes were needle sharp waiting.

"Relax. I have it safe."

Judy's impatience boiled over. "Well what's the set up? Blackmail?"

"Don't be so quick to judge others by your own standards." Randle sat down and pulled his overcoat around him. "I came to warn you that you'd better find some other source of income."

Judy thought fast. Randle's tongue was hanging out: he was panting for it. All she had to do was string Randle along. The scam was too perfect to abandon and it taught men a lesson – giving her a delicious feeling of power and control.

Judy came and sat beside him, making sure her red dress rode up at the hip. "Thank you for tipping me off. I'm sorry I misjudged you. You meet so many creeps in my line of work. A real man makes a refreshing change."

"I hoped you'd see it that way. But I'm not a fool. Don't pretend any rapid switch of affections from Karl to me. When it happens I want it to be real and for keeps."

"You're sure of yourself aren't you?"

Randle nodded. "Sure, and determined, ruthless and unstoppable. I know what I want and how I'm going to get it."

Judy sensed an invisible net being sprung and involuntarily flinched. "Let's take it nice and slow at the moment. You're bewildering me."

"No I'm not. You're just calculating the odds. Think about it."

Randle rose and tightened the belt of his raincoat. "I have to speak to your boyfriend. But that needn't trouble you." And he left.

An hour later Karl reappeared and dumped a carrier bag full of wine and beer in the kitchen. "There, that should keep us stocked up. By the way, I just saw Randle," he called back to Judy from the kitchen.

"Oh yes?" she replied, warily.

Then Karl came through to join her. "I don't know what he's up to. He seemed so hot on the case at the trial. I thought my time was up then. But now he seems to have gone cold on the whole thing. I don't think he's dug up any new leads. He talked about seeing Todd but I can't see Todd telling him any more than he told me."

"Then why not let it drop? You've been acquitted. Put it behind you and make a fresh start with me."

Karl grinned at the reversal, with Judy giving him his own advice back again. Then he became determined again. "I know what you're saying makes sense. But I can't stop. I'll never have peace of mind till I know who the murderer is. Only then will Gloria – and you – be safe."

"Me?"

"He's only killed women I've known. In the past that's meant only older women than you. But . . ."

". . . But since you've taken up with younger women the killer may too? It's fantastic."

"Is it? Anyway, I've got to see this thing through till the killer's behind bars."

Talk of prison reminded Judy of her own predicament. "Do shut up about murders and prison bars."

"Well, what would you like to talk about?"

Judy moved closer, her voice dropped: "Us!"

Karl heard the sound of wedding bells and regretted his rash proposal. Marriage was not his style at all. Flitting from flower to flower, tasting their sweetness then moving on.

He knew how to charm women, make them laugh, get them into bed, but that's where it ended. Relationships were a closed book to him.

Closeness made him want to get lost for a while, just disappear off up into his cave in the hills and get high on whatever was handy.

Judy was waiting.

Karl edged away. "There's plenty of time for us."

"Oh I see, you've gone cold on me already?" she cut back at him. "Had second thoughts because I've been a bad girl?"

"No. I'm crazy about you, you know that. It's just, what's the rush?"

"And I thought you were the romantic one."

Karl's gaze became stony. "Judy don't put all this on me now. I've had things up to here. I need space."

"Well there's plenty of space out there," she blazed. "The whole world's waiting for you. I'm sure Gloria's arms are ever open."

"Don't drag Gloria into all this."

"Why not? You only really like older women, don't you? You just want to take."

"What about you? Don't push me: I'm not one of your clients."

"So that's it. I've had enough of this. Go on, clear out."

"Don't worry I'm going, I need some air."

"Well take all you need and don't hurry back."

"I come and go as I please."

"Oh do what you like." Judy decamped to her bedroom and slammed the door behind her.

Sullenly Karl let himself out.

Chapter Ten

Judy had her claws out and wasn't about to let Karl go. After more flare-ups and then reconciliations, finally it was Karl and Judy's wedding day. Gloria had boycotted the affair and Karl was dreading that at any moment he would hear of a suicide attempt by her, hoax or otherwise.

Sarah, a reluctant bridesmaid, was wandering about the flat in a dream, stunned by the unexpected turn and speed of events. She tried deep breathing to remain calm and composed but the image of Karl walking down the aisle with Judy made her want to cry.

Judy was flushed and excited at landing her man on, she felt, her terms. They would live temporarily in her flat living her way of life – that was how she saw it. Of course, Karl was terribly handsome and would look the perfect consort in the morning suit she had insisted upon. Everyone envied Karl his cool, his elusive attractiveness, his spontaneity, that touch of recklessness. Now she had it all to herself and they would envy her too.

Judy was resplendent in a full white wedding dress, cut daringly low at the top, sweeping down to accentuate the long flow of her figure. The train spread out after her like a sensuous river, which kept Sarah occupied arranging and untangling. Judy's black hair lay in glossy profusion over her high shoulders, and she wore pearls and gold earrings, but her greatest ornaments were her darting, sparkling green eyes. She was queen for the day.

Sarah's eyes were downcast trying not to resent the supporting role into which she was cast by Judy. Her own dress was a delicate peach with puff sleeves that showed off her arms and her complexion.

At last the car arrived and whisked them off to the church. Judy

53

was delighted by her first sight of Karl inside, his formal attire giving him a gallant air even if he did look uncomfortable. But her heart sank at the sight of his best man: Gary. Despite her protestations of unsuitability Karl had resisted and there was Gary, his body-building frame squeezed into a morning suit which was a comic book travesty of Karl's sophisticated elegance. With his protuberant eyes frantically scanning the aisle for her entrance, he looked like Billy Bunter on speed.

Sighing, she took a deep breath and then donned her biggest winning smile which she would maintain all the way to the altar if it killed her.

The guests were a motley collection: old friends carelessly lost touch with but hastily reassembled by Judy. Since loner Karl's long succession of middle-aged lovers were obviously taboo, Judy had forced on him Todd and his cronies to make up the numbers.

Judy looked radiant as her vows rang out, and Karl somehow got through it. Formality and commitments were new to him and he had to fight a dizzying impulse to race back down the aisle and away to the hills.

What was he doing? The question buzzed around his head. Judy was so stunning, alluring,that the answer seemed obvious and yet he could not picture what their life together would be like ten minutes hence never mind ten years.

But he couldn't have gone on the way he had, carelessly messing up his own and other's lives. He had lived selfishly, finding sexual satisfaction where he could, and then suddenly he'd be gone. He didn't want to end up a joke, a middle-aged Casanova, without achievement or profession.

He believed Judy when she said she'd make something of him, something to be proud of. She herself was so dazzling that when she turned it on she bewitched him: under her spell he couldn't see anyone else. It was only when she became bored, irritable, distracted and seemed to forget his very existence in favour of more glamorous dreams that he found himself free to think of other people.

At the reception Todd waddled up beside him. "Your father would have been proud."

Karl's brow creased. "Would he? Well thank God he's not here to ruin it."

Todd tut-tutted, then continued unabashed: "You've a fine girl there, turn any man's eye. What a beauty! You're a lucky man. She could really help you. We are talking riches if you play your cards right. I could put some business your way if you'd only listen."

"I don't want riches, and I don't like your business."

"But Judy does. Now what about it? Share out your father's hidden fortune and you've hit the jack-pot. Remember she won't sit around for ever waiting for the good times to roll, believe me."

Karl turned away and went to find another drink. Conversation with Todd was always distasteful. But it was certainly true that Judy liked a fast life-style. The question was: how to give it to her?

"Penny for them?"

Karl looked up and Sarah was in front of him proffering a glass of champagne. Gratefully he accepted and drank half a glass straight down.

"Hey, steady on, you've a speech to make yet, remember?"

"A speech." Karl groaned, and Sarah laughed at his panic-stricken features.

"Oh, it won't be so bad. Just remember to tell Judy how beautiful she looks and thank everyone."

Karl nodded. "You make it sound so easy. Still the bit about Judy won't be hard. She is stunning isn't she?"

They both looked across at her, regal in her richly cut wedding dress with the silk and lace.

"You have to give her that."

Karl heard the reluctance in Sarah's voice.

Sarah looked down. "Oh, listen to me. How ungracious can you get. Go on, get away before I make a fool of myself."

Karl looked into her melting expression, those luminous hazel eyes which made him want to swim in them. "I've made a mistake. I should have married you," he blurted out.

Sarah turned away. "No, I've made you say that with a couple of tears. It's an old trick. I despise myself. You've married the right sister."

Karl grasped her by the shoulders, then released her as other guests moved in their direction. "I mean it," he hissed. "You've always been there for me like my good angel."

"Yes but I'm supposed to be Judy's good angel too. I can't be that for both of you. It's tearing me apart. Oh leave me alone," and she ran away to the ladies room.

Karl was left stranded, bewildered. Why had he said that? Did he mean it? What a mess.

On the other side of the room Todd sidled up to Judy, who was giddy, basking in the glory of the moment.

"Have you come to tell me I'm stunning?" she began coquettishly.

"You are always that. It doesn't need a beautiful wedding dress to convince me of that."

"I'll give you this Harold, you do know what to say to a girl."

"Ah, but if only you had let actions speak louder than words."

Judy tried to hide her revulsion by a broad grin. "You older men, you're all the same. Besides, I bet you have a string of young girls."

This was cruelly untrue and Harold's mouth tensed in a line of pain. Then he forced himself to be amiable again. "Anyway, I see you've picked yourself a young stallion. He should keep you warm on cold winter nights."

"I've no complaints," and a gleam came into her laughing eyes.

"Mind you," Todd continued, "I gather it has been a cosy little threesome up in your flat since the trial. My imagination has been working overtime over that."

Judy bridled: "I bet it has. Now don't go too far Harold." Her fist was ready.

"Heaven forfend. I merely speak as I find. By the way where is the lucky man now? He was over there with Sarah a minute ago."

Her attention directed, Judy saw Karl disconsolately staring at the carpet. This was not the behaviour she expected of her bridegroom on their wedding day and she was about to go across and upbraid him when Todd stopped her.

"He's had a bit of a shock, that's all. He'll be all right in a minute."

"What are you on about? And where's Sarah? I need her to circulate."

"Well she's had a bit of a shock too."

Judy's eyes narrowed. "Harold, what are you up to? If you've been pressurising Karl about money on my wedding day I'll brain you. I've told you before: leave him to me. He'll soon get the taste for the good life, and besides he can refuse me nothing – or I might start refusing him something!"

"Well said. You always did have spirit. And I'm glad we think alike about this. But no: I was thinking of something else."

"What?"

"Well I overheard Karl tell Sarah that he'd married the wrong sister. Highly embarrassing to hear and of course said in a rash moment with the champagne gone to his head."

"He said that? On my wedding day. It was Sarah, she battered those eyelashes at him, so demurely, I bet."

"Well yes, she did seem to be simpering up to him, so perhaps it's best put down to her fault."

Judy was drinking champagne rapidly, and seething, twisting this way and that, so that her train became entangled.

"Oh damn this dress. I wish I'd never seen it. Karl, I'll strangle him. You can't make a man say a thing like that."

But Todd intervened, quickly turning her away from prying eyes. "Now, now, you take my advice and play this cagey. It's your day, don't let these hyenas feast on it by making a scene. You don't want to be a laughing stock, do you?"

Judy shook the wild tears from her eyes, mascara smudged.

"You listen to your Uncle Harold. Don't let on to Karl you know. It may be a misunderstanding, silly words he regrets already. And if not, well you're in a better position to have your revenge if he doesn't suspect anything. You get my drift?"

Judy nodded, then her head came up. She was still fuming. "Oh, whether he meant it or not, he'll pay for it. No one treats me with contempt behind my back and gets away with it. He'll suffer for it, mark my words."

"That's my girl. Between us we'll wrap him around our little fingers."

Judy stopped him. "Hang on a moment, where do you come into all this?"

"I have my interest. His late father left several irons in the fire including the treasure. It's just that Karl's taken some convincing to come in with us."

Judy thought that in this, Karl had at least shown some sense, but kept it to herself. "Well that's something different. This between me and Karl is private, understand? I don't want it spreading around."

"Of course. I'm the soul of discretion. I only meant that it might serve our common interest at some point to act in concert."

Judy saw that she needed to buy Todd's silence with at least some vague agreement. "We can work together, Harold."

"That's all I wanted to know. I felt maybe you'd held that other unfortunate business against me."

Judy pretended surprise. "You mean when we were drugged and then raped?"

"Shush, keep your voice down. Don't say such a thing. He was only a business acquaintance who said he wanted a bit of fun. How was I to know he was going to turn out to be an animal? After all, you'd been an escort before."

"So it was none of your fault then?"

"Well, you weren't exactly wet behind the ears. And there were two of you."

"Thanks a lot, that's very comforting."

"Oh, you know what I mean. Anyway what's the point in arguing. It was a dreadful experience for all concerned. I lost money on that deal, you know. So let's forget it, put it behind us."

"Well of all the bare-faced effrontery!" Todd's cold-bloodedness turned her stomach. "Go away. I like to choose the company I keep."

"All right, but think on. My business won't wait for ever." Todd then walked off to round up his cronies and press one of them to buy him a double whisky at the bar.

That Judy, Todd mused, she was so fiery and independent it was going to be tricky manipulating Karl through her. But he'd made a start.

Chapter Eleven

"Well this is a fine start to married life," Judy muttered to herself as she opened the door to the flat, coming home early and separately from her honeymoon.

She wished now she had thrown his confession to Sarah back in his face. Anything would have been better than the sulking, and avoiding looks, the flare-ups and disappointments. Paris should have been 'so romantic': instead Paris had been a nightmare. Karl didn't want to sight-see, but Karl didn't want to stay in; all he really wanted to do was frequent boring jazz clubs till the early hours, which gave her a headache.

So she'd left him a note and come home early. That would serve him right, and maybe shock him into action. After all he was her husband, damn it, and he'd better start behaving like one. She wasn't losing out to her doe-eyed sister with her seductive ways.

"Hello," came a calm, self-possessed voice.

Judy spun round, dropping her suitcase in amazement. "Sarah! What on earth are you doing here?"

"I live here, remember? You weren't due back for a fortnight yet. What's happened?"

Judy was defensive, awkward. "Oh, nothing. Paris was gruesome, that's all."

"So where's Karl?"

"Probably under a table with a woman in some terrible jazz club, I expect."

Sarah came forward and embraced her sister.

Hypocrite, Judy thought.

"So you two had a row?"

"More an undeclared war."

Judy wrenched off her coat and threw it across the room.

"Oh." Sarah didn't know what to say.

"If you hadn't batted your eyelids at Karl none of this would have happened."

"But I didn't"

"At my wedding of all days you conniving bitch."

Sarah's mouth set in a small hard line. "Now you just hold it right there. You were the one who said we should share him, and take him down a peg or two."

Judy was angry at being reminded, of being caught out. "Well that was before. I didn't know you were going to move in on him on my wedding day and try and take him for yourself."

"For the last time, I didn't. It was Karl who said he'd chosen the wrong sister. I didn't encourage him. I think he regretted it as soon as he said it. You've nothing to worry about."

Judy snorted. "A husband I can't be sure of. Who let me come all the way home from my honeymoon alone. And you say I've nothing to worry about?"

"I mean it can all be put right. You'll twist him round your little finger."

"Will I now? It looks the opposite to me. He's set us against each other and we swore no one would ever do that."

"I know. I tried to stand together with you as always, but your marriage seemed to alter the whole picture."

"Why?"

"Oh come on. What were we going to have: a rota?"

"I'm not sure I want him now."

"You're just saying that." Sarah gave Judy a knowing look. "You want him all right. You never let go of something once you've really got your claws into it."

"What a pretty picture of me you paint. At least I don't sneak around behind people's backs."

Sarah was pleading, desperate. "Why won't you believe me? I've not been deceiving you with Karl. I'm not that devious."

"Oh, aren't you madam? Well I'm not going to sit around to find out. Pack your bags and go clear away from here."

"If you'd noticed I was gathering up my things anyway." Sarah's tone was icy. "You merely caught me unawares, coming back early. Another fortnight and I would have been gone. I don't want to play gooseberry."

"Well hurry up about it. I don't want Karl barging in and finding you still here."

"If you were any good for him you'd have no reason to worry," Sarah said quickly, retreating to her bedroom to find her things.

Judy was furious and yet half afraid that this might be true. Thrown off balance she could only strut up and down impotently while Sarah finished her packing and carried her belongings to the door. Judy was seeing Sarah off her patch, but it was Sarah who retained her self command. She knew her sister too well.

"Key!" Judy rasped and held out her hand.

"Oh really, " Sarah protested more in pity than anger and handed it over. "Don't shut me out of your life. You might need me some day."

"Hardly," and Judy slammed the door on Sarah's retreating figure.

She had the flat to herself: and never had she felt so alone. What had she done? Sarah, her one good angel, her true better self, gone. Judy felt as if part of her had died.

Who would she confide in? Who would care for her more than she did for herself? Who would hold her back from disaster? Who would understand her, and still love her, now?

Karl, half a day behind Judy in returning, was lugging his suitcase around town putting off the moment of confrontation. That damn note. Did Judy know about his blurted confession to Sarah? How could she? Sarah wouldn't have told her – that would be inviting trouble.

But his own guilt and mixed up feelings had distorted every moment in Paris. Any hint of annoyance, any petulant refusal by Judy he had construed as a danger signal.

Unable to relax they had worn out each other's nerves till flare-ups were almost an hourly occurrence. He needed peace, balm right now, a sympathetic shoulder: Sarah in fact.

Uncertain of his reception, and whether he should be doing this at all, nevertheless he sought her out at the greenhouses and eventually found her.

Sarah looked up from compressing some seeds into a grow-box. "Before you say anything Karl, I've spoken to Judy. She knows everything."

"Oh hell!"

"She more or less threw me out, which I suppose is understandable from her point of view."

Karl scowled at her. "Why do you always have to be so damned understanding and reasonable? Here am I going out of my head and you talk so calmly."

"Do I?" She stopped her work and looked at him. Underneath her dirtied lamb's-wool sweater her breast rose and fell with increasing rapidity. "Only because I try, I feel I ought. It's not because I want to."

Karl grabbed her and kissed her passionately. "I've wanted to do that ever since I got back from Paris."

Sarah, despite her good intentions, responded hungrily and then drew back. "This is wrong Karl. Judy and me sharing you started as a bit of a giggle but it's got all out of hand now. All our feelings are running too high. It will destroy us unless we stop."

Karl held her face fiercely in his hands. "Never. It's you I want. Judy was just like some fever with me. Always trying to drag me down with her."

"That's just talk. Judy only likes to think she lives on the wild side."

"Yes, but she never knows where to stop. All the time we were in Paris she kept hinting at some jobs Todd had lined up for us. Now there is only one sort of job that Todd puts on offer."

Sarah drew close to him again. "She didn't tell me. Stay away from Todd. He ruins lives – I know."

Karl passed his hand over her hair. "I hate him for that. The thought of anyone hurting you makes me so mad."

"No: we must be careful. Let things cool down, and then maybe we'll be able to see a way forward."

"Then you want to be with me?" Karl responded eagerly.

"I won't do anything to hurt Judy – anything more than I have already," she added with shame and regret.

And then she blurted out: "Oh I wish I had the strength to tell you to go. Why did you have to walk into out lives? Why did you have to pick out Gloria of all people in the first place?"

Karl couldn't answer this torrent of questions. Instead he took her in his arms and tried to comfort her. It was a new experience for him.

Then be picked up his suitcase and went out with a heavy heart to face up to Judy and resume their fractured life together.

Chapter Twelve

Edgy together, Judy and Karl had called an ominous truce. Sometimes passion would overtake both of them and they would wonder how they could ever have looked at anybody else. But even then their lovemaking would become a sort of fight for supremacy and power: Judy using her wiles, her slyness, Karl his bony physical strength.

Often it did them good to get out of the flat. A fast drive cleared their heads and joined them in the love of physical activity and speed. Karl admired Judy's Ferrari and wondered how she could have afforded it. But he knew where that train of thought led and tried to think of something else.

One day Judy suggested a drive and as usual Karl willingly agreed. He had no fixed employment – a vexed question between them – and was free to accept her offer.

They circled the countryside around the town for a while, carefully avoiding the village where Gloria lived. Judy's mother had been strangely silent these last few weeks. Karl even wondered guiltily if she were dead – perhaps lying there undiscovered, unclaimed. But he couldn't face going there to find out and risking the village's lynch mob again.

Back in town Judy said she was tired and pulled the Ferrari into the kerb. They sat, Judy unusually smoking a cigarette. Conversation was desultory and Karl noticed a peculiar tension in Judy.

Also she was flushed, nervous with an excited tilt to her head. He didn't flatter himself that at this precise moment he was the cause.

She seemed to be waiting for something. But what, he

wondered? It was a normal high street, full of unexciting chain stores. Nothing to get worked up about. But Judy was becoming ever more on edge, and now looking up and down the road in anticipation.

"Judy, what is the matter with you? You're as nervous as a cat."

"Very funny. Will you be quiet. I can't concentrate."

"On what?"

"Shush."

Irritated, Karl began to look up and down too, trying to see what she was interested in. Then he opened the car door.

Judy leant across and grabbed it shut. "Stay here!"

"I beg your pardon?"

"Don't get out of the car. Whatever you do."

She gunned the engine.

"Judy, please. Explain."

"I can't. There isn't time. Just sit tight." And she grinned, luxuriating in being in charge, with a marvellous secret to herself.

"Why? I don't see . . ."

"You don't have to see. I'll do all the thinking. That's my department."

Karl felt that Judy was presuming a lot but realised this wasn't the time to argue: she wasn't listening, her whole body intent, waiting for something to break.

And then it did: alarm bells, men running, and then those same men piling into the Ferrari. "Drive, drive," yelled one of the men, garish, wearing a halloween mask.

Judy didn't need telling twice; she let in the clutch and the car roared away in the blink of an eye. Within fifty yards she had turned the car down a side road out of view of the high street.

Then it was hurtling down a carefully planned route of one-way streets and little used roads till they reached a deserted and forlorn garage forecourt outside of town. Long abandoned, its battered buildings made a perfect rendezvous.

From behind a wrecked petrol pump, Todd emerged beaming a broad, satisfied smile.

"That's my girl. And you've brought a passenger. Karl, most welcome. Glad you're one of us now."

Karl opened his mouth to protest, then closed it again. There didn't seem to be any point. He had been suckered and he knew it.

Karl was left cooling his heels while frenzied discussions went on all around him. Stolen jewellery was passed across to Todd and his confederates and further instructions issued. Then the group split up into different cars and Karl was left with Judy on the desolate spot. Overgrown with weeds, panels missing from the forecourt canopy, windows smashed in the cabin, it cast a depressing, hopeless pall over their conversation.

Judy shivered. "Come on, let's clear out of this place it gives me the creeps."

"You just hold on." Karl faced her squarely, his hands plunged into his leather jacket pockets. "First you hijack me into this caper and then you expect me docilely to follow you to the car. Well you picked the wrong fella."

"All right, stay here in this god-forsaken spot and wait for the police to pick you up. It's your choice."

"If they did I'd have quite a story to tell them."

"With your record? Still I might have guessed you'd turn out to be a grass."

Karl walked smartly up to her and raised his hand. Automatically Judy's went up to protect herself and he grabbed her hand in his.

"Don't you ever accuse me of that again. I've never grassed on anyone in my life. I just don't like being used, that's all." He released her hand and angrily she snatched it back.

"Besides," he went on, "you must be mad using your Ferrari on a getaway like that. Why didn't you just advertise?"

Judy looked contemptuous. She was going to call him 'craven' but thought better of it. "There's no excitement without risk. But I'm not stupid. I switched number plates and covered the rear with masking tape. But the real trick is in the speed – I timed it: I was off that High Street in twenty seconds. No one was going to recognise us in that time – we'd just be a blur. It's all in the acceleration."

Karl watched her in amazement: she must live in fantasy land, he thought, picturing herself as some experienced, high speed getaway driver. Whereas all she really knew about was interior design and kinky blackmail.

"This was the last, the one and only time, I go on a job with you," Karl told her.

Judy became petulant, hand on her hips. "What's the matter

with you? Where's your guts? I thought you wanted excitement, like me. But all I hear is excuses. You're a total wimp."

"Take that back, and don't talk so stupid. We're not Bonny and Clyde. You brag just like my father. He spent most of his adult life slopping out behind bars."

Disconcerted Judy shifted her weight on to her other foot. "Oh please! Lighten up. It doesn't have to be like that. Two or three lucrative jobs and then we can live a life of luxury."

It was Karl's turn to smile contemptuously. "You really ought to hear yourself. It's never enough. We'd get caught. Or Todd would rat on us; he'd sell his own mother."

"Oh Todd's all right," Judy muttered, more to convince herself than anything. "Anyway, come on, pessimist. Are you riding with me or what?"

"What choice do I have?"

"None."

"Well then. Let's go. The longer we stay here the bigger the hole we're in gets."

Judy suddenly turned on him, "I'm getting awfully sick of your dark little sayings. If you can't cheer up, shut up," and she stomped off to the car.

"Bitch," he hurled after her as he followed.

"I damn well hope so."

Chapter Thirteen

Randle sat hunched over a rapidly cooling cup of coffee, biting his nails. With grim satisfaction he looked around him at the grease-stained tables, the fake wood panelling, the plastic condiments, and the garish pink strip lighting. It would serve Judy right to be dragged down to this level, to the kind of place in which he'd spent most of his working life. She needed a lesson in the hard realities.

Where was she? Women were always late, always keeping him waiting. Mentally he went over the facts for the umpteenth time, the cards that he had to play. A spiteful smile came to his lips: his hand was much better than last time, he had more leverage, she'd be more panicky. Now was the time to pull her down from her disdainful position and make her see how indispensable he was to her.

Just then she entered, pushing aside the bead curtain with an impatient flourish. He saw her lip curl and she proceeded down the main aisle like a queen visiting the slums.

Her gaze fell on him. "Randle. Why have you dragged me to this hole?"

He made way for her on the bench seat: "Sit here, keep your voice down. Even these places have ears."

Sullenly Judy complied. Her black leather dress rode up and Randle admired her long, slender legs.

"All right, stop ogling me. What's so important?"

Randle had to admit that nothing fazed her. "Remember my old police dossier on you?"

"Oh that," and Judy tossed her hair back so that it fell carelessly over her shoulders.

"I took it with me when I left the force."

Involuntarily Judy laughed, breaking the tension. "Big deal."

Randle felt insulted. "Don't talk to me like that. You're this close to a long jail term," and he held finger and thumb inches apart. "I've half a mind to put you there."

Judy turned away from him. "With your half a mind you couldn't put anyone anywhere," she sniffed.

He grabbed her by the shoulders, and his face – careworn, disappointed, angry – bore down on hers. "Where do you get off being so high and mighty? Are you too stupid to see you're facing years in jail?"

"Me? For a little sex ploy with clients who'd never testify against me. You must be joking."

"Not just that," Randle muttered impatiently. "You've gone up a league. Driving a getaway car for a jewel robbery. Half a million in stones I heard."

Judy blanched. Her superior smile became fixed, her eyes wide, desperate. "How much?" she let slip.

Randle leant back a little, appearing to relax now he was in control.

"What do you want?"

Dreamily he answered, "I want you, and no Karl in the way." Then recovering himself he went on: "Using your Ferrari to impress Karl. That really was stupid. What were you thinking of?"

Judy hung her head. "I'm an expert driver. We were only seconds on the High Street. How did you know?"

"All right, I was half guessing, but I've been on your trail for ages. I was bound to catch up with you sooner or later."

Sobered, Judy sat with her hands in her lap. "So what happens now? Blackmail, or are you turning me over?"

"Now listen to me. I'm in charge now. You do exactly what I tell you, when I tell you, and I might, just might, get you out of all this."

"Yes, but why?"

"I told you before, I've plans for you and me. Big plans – and they don't include your friend Karl."

"Oh him," and already Karl seemed discarded.

"Well?"

Dazed, Judy nodded.

"Right. Karl becomes our fall guy. He was in the getaway car, wasn't he? So we make a statement to the police saying that he stole your car and drove it alone that day. The police are itching to put him away for something after he was acquitted for murder. Then we disappear. Karl's left high and dry."

"But he'll deny it, accuse me."

"So, who'll believe him? With his record and my credentials he'll go down for it."

"I don't know."

"Listen, it's you or him, take your choice."

Judy frowned. She thought of Karl – then, with Sarah: 'Married the wrong sister.' He'd find out how true that was. This could be the final revenge for his betrayal of her.

"All right. Let's do it. You sort out the details."

"Good. And don't shed any tears over Karl. He's a killer who got away with murder. You'll only be safe when he's behind bars."

Judy didn't bother to argue. Instead she half rose. "I've got to go now." And she slid along the bench seat. She found Randle's company for any length of time a strain on her nerves.

Randle's hand held her back. "Oh, one last thing. Don't get any silly ideas about using me till you're out of the frame and Karl's a memory, and then dumping me. After this we're inseparable. I've got enough on you to keep us together for ever. Don't worry," he patted her face roughly, "you'll get to like me, love me. I'm really a loveable guy."

Chapter Fourteen

Judy was in a highly excitable state as she waited to go to Todd's for the share-out. What if Todd guessed that she was taking the money and running with Randle? Karl might bring the roof down on all of them who were left. Still, that wasn't her problem.

Before Randle muscled in on her it had all seemed so glamorous. Like being a racing driver. It was so different from the tawdry world of sex and money. Clean, exciting, getaway driving sharpened the wits, and pitted her against machine, time, and people. She had come out on top – till now.

Randle was on to her, and how long before others followed? It was only a matter of time, as he'd said. No, she had to swallow it, and be nice to him – very nice to him. Give him the works, flash those green eyes and use her perfectly honed body on him. Sleep with him if necessary. Clearly the obsessive type, he would need plenty of convincing and reassuring. Randle and Todd, what a pair.

She drove across town and parked in an overgrown flagged bay in front of Todd's 'surgery'.

As she pushed open the chipped wooden door she wondered how many bogus patients had gone through to the back to receive their drugs or other illegal substances. No wonder he'd been struck off: he'd been so blatant it seemed nearly the whole town had traipsed to his door.

She went on through the interior doorway until she found Todd seated as usual like a malevolent sumo wrestler behind his desk.

He motioned her to sit down.

"Where is everybody?" Judy was curious and impatient.

"Who did you have in mind?" Todd's small grey eyes seemed

heavy, guarded.

"The gang, for the shareout. I hope you've not dragged me here on a wasted journey."

"That depends." Todd slithered in his seat, to make himself comfortable.

"On what?"

"On what you were expecting. You didn't seriously think that after your little escapade with the Ferrari we'd all meet you in broad daylight and split the proceeds. The Bill could walk straight in on us and have us cold."

"So why am I here? When do I get my money?"

Todd ignored her questions. "It defies belief you know," the words disgorged slowly, "that someone of your intelligence could use a flash car of their own on a getaway."

Judy was disconcerted. "All right, it was rash, I admit it. But I did put dummy plates on and disguise the rear of the car. I wasn't totally thoughtless. I suppose I just got carried away."

"It's just one big jaunt for you, isn't it? Playing at robber to impress your fancy boyfriend. Well some of us have more to lose than you. We've got form."

"All right, I've said I'm sorry. I won't do it again."

"Too right you won't. You won't get the chance. The police have been round us all. If you talk I personally will shut your mouth for ever."

"Oh, come on Harold, you don't mean that." She forced a chilled smile at him and began to uncross her legs and move her body the way she knew he found irresistible. "You wouldn't," she purred.

"Stop doing that – wriggling about. You know I can't concentrate. You're a bad girl, you know. I should fix you for good."

"Well you can't stay angry at me for long can you, particularly when I do this?" She rose and leant across to kiss him.

Todd grabbed her impulsively and slavered over her with his kisses. Then he pushed her off. "All right, that's enough of that. You always try it on."

Judy pulled herself off him with a contrite expression. "Well of course, if you really don't want me to do this . . ." and she began to pull down the zip on her dress.

Todd's gaze was transfixed. "Judy!"

71

"There now, I knew you'd see it my way."

Later that afternoon, as she drove back to the flat Judy was shaking, close to tears. When Todd had threatened to shut her mouth for ever, she had taken him seriously. She'd never felt that frightened of him before. Going up a league had its penalties as well as compensations.

She hated herself for buying him off with her body but it was her only effective weapon. What she'd do if it ever failed her, didn't bear thinking about. Anyway Todd was pacified, glassy-eyed for the present – till it wore off.

She couldn't ignore the cordon that was moving in on her from two directions now: Randle and Todd. At least Todd didn't demand that she run away with him. Yet.

Finally she reached the flat and with nervous fingers let herself in. She needed a drink above all. As she headed for the cabinet she heard sounds coming from the bedroom.

Burglars? The Police? All sorts of possibilities sprang to her mind. She tiptoed to the door to listen but the sounds were very indistinct.

She noticed it wasn't fully closed and knelt down to peer through the crack between the edge of the door and the door jamb.

The light was on in her bedroom, clothes were scattered about, a perfume bottle of hers was on the carpet, and her bed was occupied.

She squinted to see, difficult at that angle from the bed. Then a man raised himself on his forearms, arched his back and his naked torso glistened in the artificial light. It was Karl – and underneath him reaching up gracefully to massage his chest before drawing him to her was Sarah.

Judy swayed back and then went to sit in cold fury first in a chair, and then in the car. She wanted to put as much distance between herself and them as possible. Otherwise she might just grab a blunt instrument and bludgeon both of them to death.

To wait until she was out of the way, sneak behind her back, and make love in her bed after she'd kicked Sarah out of the flat. It was insupportable, humiliating.

It had been different when she had initiated sharing Karl with Sarah. That had been like charity, throwing Sarah a well gnawed bone so that she wouldn't feel totally left out.

But now married to Karl, Judy had exclusive rights to him and Sarah knew that. Woe betide anyone who encroached on her private sexual property. He performed only for her now; that was the rule, the taboo, that was being broken at this very moment.

Wasn't she exciting, enticing, satisfying enough for him? She knew more tricks, more positions, more sex games than Sarah – so why her?

What was so special about Sarah? She couldn't bear it if Karl found Sarah more desirable than her.

Because if she had lost that power, she had lost everything. Without it she felt she was nothing.

She'd see Karl and Sarah destroyed, annihilated. Randle was right – the only solution was to disappear and leave Karl rotting in jail, his lovemaking days ended. Serve him right.

d

Chapter Fifteen

As the days went by Judy was becoming desperate. Her meetings with Randle were secret and inconclusive. They discussed various plans for her disappearance and their new life together but none of it came to anything. She felt the police net closing in on her all the time. At home she was jealous every minute she was away from Karl and the flat, with the loathsome certainty that he was using her bed to sleep with Sarah.

Somehow she hadn't been able to confront him over discovering the pair of them in bed together. It would have meant losing face and besides, they could say she had never objected before. She was caught, squirming, in a double bind and she hated it.

Repressing her emotions was new and alien to Judy, and it threw her completely off balance. She was having nightmares and becoming paranoid that people were laughing at her behind her back. None of this had happened to her before. She was frightened and she daren't admit it to anyone. After all she had paraded herself as braver, more reckless, than any man.

The rest of the time Judy and Karl were largely flung together, in mutual misunderstanding and suspicion. Karl was dreading that Judy would inveigle him into another of her suicidal criminal escapades. She sensed his silent criticism and rebelled against it.

In her turn she was scathing about what she called his 'little boy' pranks – his whisky still, his selling from a suitcase. 'Kids' stuff' she called it and asked him why he had ever bothered to come back from London with his tail between his legs.

Then he'd say he wasn't stopping to listen to this nagging and would disappear for days on end into the woods and hills, into his cave where he could be alone or hold a midnight rave with a few friends.

Judy felt excluded and insatiably curious, wondering just what exactly he was up to behind her back. She had had words with Sarah and needed to know.

One evening she drove her Ferrari to the clearing by the river where she'd parked before and began to follow the paths to the cave. Her memory and sense of direction in the countryside were poor and in the dark she stumbled about, her clothes torn, her skin scratched.

She seemed to go round in circles for hours, finally shouting out hoarsely, but no one answered. She was beside herself with anger, frustration, berating herself and Karl for undertaking such a fool's errand.

Eventually by dint of trying every path leading to the rise above, she hit on the approach to Karl's cave. Dishevelled, exhausted, out of her mind with worry, and unclear why she had come she stumbled forward.

Karl was clearing up after the night's party, lugging piles of empty bottles to a broken box by the entrance. Judy could see women's clothing scattered about, and as Karl reached for it, she shrieked: "Leave that alone, you bastard, how could you – coming up here for your orgies with women while I was left alone in the flat wondering where the hell you were?"

Karl was taken aback by her wild appearance and accusations. Was this the same Judy who believed in free love, in living life to extremes, taking it to the limit and beyond?

"Judy, come here out of the dark. How did you find me?"

"Thought I couldn't, didn't you? Well I've damn near torn my legs to bits scrabbling through all this undergrowth to track you down. You'll pay for everything you've done to me Karl."

Karl stretched out his arms towards her: "What have I done to you? I would say any fault is fifty-fifty. Come in here and sit down. Have a drink."

Judy was cold and lost and hated his calm self possession. "Damn you. I'd like to kill you. You're ruining my life."

"Come on then," he beckoned, laughing.

She clawed at him, then launched herself, all her pent up rage released. She punched, scratched, bit, tore at his clothes, kicked him in the groin.

Inflamed, Karl fought back. How had he ever become entangled with this wild, mad woman? He should have known better after his experience with her mother Gloria. Forced to defend himself, he punched her, tore her coat and trousers, and kicked her down the hill.

He came roaring down after, just after she sprang aside and clawed him again. He clipped her and then grabbed her round the waist and threw her among the rocks.

Winded, he lay there listening for further cries and curses from that direction. But all was silence apart from furtive animal rustlings. He waited on, suspicious, thinking she might rush him again unawares.

But as the minutes lengthened he went to investigate. The rocks were empty: no trace of her. He prowled around the area, called her name, and brushed the undergrowth with a stick, but did not succeed in flushing her out.

Finally he gave up and wandered back to the cave. He was concerned about Judy being out in the woods all night, but the weather was mild and she wouldn't die of exposure. She'd probably stumble back the way she'd come. Well good luck to her; he was exhausted, sore, torn, and in need of a long drink and a dreamless sleep. He collapsed onto the mattress in the cave, took a swig, and passed out.

The next morning he awoke to find the place swarming with police. Randle was bearing down on him, fist grabbing him by the shirt. "Well, what have you done with Judy?"

Karl wiped the sleep from his eyes and felt his thumping head. "Who?"

"You heard, Judy. Don't mess me about. Her sister Sarah called when she never came home from here last night. She was alarmed. Where is Judy?"

"How the hell should I know? We had an argument and she wandered off somewhere."

"Show us," and Randle dragged Karl to his feet.

In the daylight, Karl could see that he and Judy had left quite a scene of devastation. Bottles, boxes, torn clothing, were scattered about and the soft earth was churned up with great gouges where their bodies had collided.

"Down here," a voice called, and the police all decamped down to the rocks. They found blood, more torn clothing, and some personal belongings.

Randle grabbed Karl by the throat. "What have you done with her? Where is she buried?"

Karl recoiled in horror, and one of Randle's former fellow officers warned him to lay off.

"Lay off?" Randle rounded on him. "Karl beat one murder charge, and we find the bloody remnants of another woman. You tell me to lay off? I tell you he's not getting away with it again."

The police scoured the woodland, but found most of the blood and clothing concentrated round the rocks and the cave. However, there were traces along the tracks.

Randle prodded Karl in the chest. "It doesn't matter how far into the wood you dragged her body: they'll find her. They've dogs for a job like that."

The dogs were brought, then men fanned out, but no Judy was found alive or dead.

Then far into the undergrowth came a policeman's cry: "Over here."

They all converged on the spot to see the man triumphantly pointing to a hand scythe, half buried in the fern, its blade covered in blood stains.

Randle turned to Karl with smug satisfaction. "Well that about clinches it, don't you think? You didn't throw it far enough. Go on, why don't you take him in?"

Chapter Sixteen

As Karl waited for his visitors he felt that nothing could surprise him now. Whatever Todd and Gloria had come to say could not be more weird and disconcerting than the events of the last few weeks.

Ever since that dawn when the police, egged on by Randle, had dragged him from his cave hideaway on suspicion of murder, Karl had been bombarded by hostile accusations, including his own. He was desperately worried about Judy. Was she alive or dead? It had been a horrendous fight and she had collided with that rocky outcrop at high speed. Her skull could have been crushed, she could have wandered off to die somewhere. But then where was the body?

Before she had arrived he had been high on drink and 'ecstasy'. The rave had been pretty wild and his memory of events was hazy. But the bloodstained scythe: he did not remember using it at all. Certainly it was his, for keeping down the gorse that encroached upon the cave, but he had never used it in anger.

Maybe he had carelessly dropped the scythe down among the rocks and Judy had sliced her head open on it.

She had flown at him like a wild animal, trying to claw him with her bare hands, but still he needed to know she was safe. Underneath her brashness she was vulnerable he felt, and needed his protection.

Often he despaired of his situation: Judy terribly injured or dead and the police ferociously keen to prove he had killed her. Randle and the rest were still smarting from his acquittal over the original serial killings and were determined that he should go down for this one. He could see them gloating over his lack of alibi, the undeniable evidence of Judy's presence at the cave and the bloody struggle.

Yet like hungry wolves they were frustrated at the end: her body refused to turn up. So, angry, they circled him baying for a confession. But he could not say 'I killed her' because he did not know.

He had never felt lonelier in his life. The uncertainty gnawed at him. It had done terrible things to him before the last trial and he didn't think he could stand the agony repeated all over again. Karl felt cruelly deprived of the one person a man could normally lean on: his wife.

He'd been utterly abandoned, and hesitated to raise his hopes by expecting anything of Todd and Gloria's visit. But at least they'd come.

When signalled he rose, the prison garb feeling itchy against his skin. He'd never get used to it.

Down institutional corridors smelling of disinfectant and cheap polish he was walked to the visiting room.

It was off-putting suddenly to be shooed into a vast gymnasium-type room full of canteen tables and milling visitors and prisoners. He hated crowds and prison forced them upon him.

Overcoming his distaste he sat down, with Gloria and Todd opposite. Gloria wore a long blue flounced coat with imitation fur collar and a gardenia in her buttonhole. The scent knocked him sick for a moment and made him think of Sarah and assignations with her behind the greenhouses.

Todd sat impassive, watchful, weighing up prison's effect on Karl. He sported a brown double-breasted suit with wide lapels, a striped tie, and brogues.

Gloria gripped Karl's hand impulsively and squeezed it too hard: "I should scold you unmercifully for ditching me but I haven't the heart when I see you here."

Karl retrieved his crushed hand. "Very good of you," he mumbled sarcastically. And then more loudly, confidently, "still, thanks for coming," to both of them.

Todd nodded and acknowledged with a lazy wave of his hand, as if graciousness came naturally to him.

"But why, Karl? What's happened to Judy?" Gloria pleaded.

Karl explained the facts as far as he could remember them.

"And that's it? A scuffle, Judy falls head over heels down a hillock and the police call it murder? They've got to be joking."

"They are not doing that Gloria. I'm going down like the *Titanic*."

Gloria shushed him: "Don't talk like that: it's so defeatist. I can't bear it. Tell him Harold."

Todd cleared his throat. "If you'll play ball . . ."

"Oh no, Harold, not all that rigmarole again. I thought you promised."

Todd glared at her: "If Karl wants my help please let me put it in my own way. And stop interrupting."

Gloria, silenced, went into a huff.

Todd resumed, leaning forward, fixing Karl with small grey eyes. "Cards on the table: you're in a terrible hole. You were there, a fight ensued, blood everywhere, Judy's body disappeared. You'll need the best barrister money can buy. So for the last time: tell me where your father's fortune is buried and I'll fix up the barrister. I can't say fairer than that."

Karl exploded: "Fairer than that? I don't need you to find me a brief. I'll do it myself. I keep telling you, there isn't any fortune. It's all a figment of your imagination."

"Don't insult me son. Your father told me, and the proceeds of the last job were never recovered. Come on, what have you to lose? You can't spend the money in jail."

Karl dragged back his chair. "I've had enough. I don't have to listen to this. You're not bothered about what happened to Judy. I'm going back to my cell."

"No Karl, don't. Stay, for my sake, just a few minutes. You don't know how I've missed you," and Gloria's desperate, outreaching hand caressed Karl's face. "You should never have married Judy even if she is my own flesh and blood daughter. I was the right one for you: I would have cared for you."

Inevitably, Karl was reminded of those similar words he had spoken to Sarah at his wedding reception. "I can't help the past Gloria. I'm worried sick about Judy. Don't you care what happened to her?"

"Of course. But I know you didn't harm her. I'm going mad without you."

"Gloria, I can't stand any more of this. It's doing my head in."

Gloria was suddenly shamed. "I'm sorry," she said, "you

locked up in here and I'm going on at you. Never could hold my tongue could I? I love you Karl, I always will. But I'll go now. I'll see if I can talk some sense into Harold here."

"Now Gloria," Harold remonstrated.

"Harold, shut up. We must do everything to help Karl and that includes you."

"Don't push it, Gloria," and suddenly there was a steely warning look in his eye. "You think over what I said, young Karl. Let me know when you're ready to do a deal. But don't leave it too long. Good barristers are hard to find. Like buried treasure."

Chapter Seventeen

"Guilty!"

This time it was no bad dream; though Karl, utterly bewildered, angry, felt it must be.

It was déjà vu gone wrong; he had watched the foreman of the jury rise just as in his previous trial. He had heard the request from the judge, "Have you reached a verdict upon which you are all agreed?" The foreman had assented and the judge asked for their verdict.

So far the replay was perfect, but then it went terribly wrong: 'guilty', wasn't the verdict, it couldn't be. He was no more guilty this time than last. Unless – and a terrible thought seared through him for a split second – he was equally guilty as he had been last time.

No, no, he battered at himself, it couldn't be. He wasn't that kind of person, a murderer.

But his thoughts, feelings, were immaterial now. The judge was telling him he'd been found guilty of manslaughter, since there was no evidence of premeditation, and he was sentenced to ten years in prison.

Ten years: the sentence rocked Karl. Remand had been hell, locked away from the hills and the caves, the wine bars and female company he loved so much. But ten years: he'd go crazy.

Then rough hands were taking him down. Randle was there to greet him with a malicious grin on his face. "Well we finally nailed you, you bastard. Only by rights it would have been for all those other killings too and you'd be put away for life. Still at your age it feels like life doesn't it? You'll be like an old man when you get out. Prison does that to you. Then no woman will look at you."

Karl stared back at him in baffled incredulity. "Keep away from me. Why do you hate me? I never did anything to you or anyone."

"Oh didn't you? Take him out of my sight."

As he was hauled away, Karl called back in desperation, "I'll get you for this. It's a set-up. The truth will come out one day."

Karl was then manhandled from room to room, all the same to him, institutional grey, functional cigarette scarred tables, broken chairs.

He had lost his future. All plans were null and void. His attempt at coming home after the high life in London had gone sour and brought nothing but tragedy. He had entered free-fall and had now hit rock bottom.

Where was Judy? It was a terrible anguish to him not to know what had become of her. Certainly he'd hurt her in the struggle, but surely not fatally. But if not, where in heaven's name was she? Why hadn't she come forward? Had she staggered off to die, falling in some river or lonely ravine, or had some savage man finished off what he, Karl, had started?

He hated to think of Judy's lovely body, battered and abused, lying twisted in some rain-soaked ditch somewhere, unclaimed. She had loved life so, super-charged, vibrant.

Later his half-brother Gary came to visit and made game, naïve attempts to cheer him up. "Do you want to see my Spiderman impression again?"

"Not really," and Karl dropped his tired head.

Seeing that Gary was lost he took pity on him. "Go on then, do your bug-eyed monster."

Gary's eyes lit up and he capered in his seat, half rising, till a warder with raised eyes motioned to him to sit still.

"Everyone sends their love and regards," Gary hastened to tell him, and then stopped embarrassed.

"Really? I feel like the forgotten man in here. God knows when I'll ever get out."

"You will, you'll see."

Karl looked at him again. Gary looked different: he was filling out, and he seemed even more pop-eyed than usual.

"Is Todd feeding you steroids?"

"Karl, you know . . ."

"Gary, don't lie to me. You never have and you've no talent for it. Yes or no?"

Gary was shame-faced, head down. "Yes. But listen Karl, I need them. I couldn't build my body into this without them. And I'm careful, I don't over-do them."

Karl clenched his fists in frustration. He knew his half-brother. "I wish I was there to keep an eye on you. You've probably been eating them like sweets."

"Karl, that's not fair. I'm not an imbecile, you know. Todd thinks highly of me. He's given me more responsible jobs now."

"That's another thing. I wish you'd get away from that man. He's a bad influence on you."

"Todd? He's done everything for me."

"At a price. There's always a price with Todd. And one day you won't be able to pay it."

Gary felt rebuffed. "If you feel that way I'm not sure I should pass on the message."

"So now we're getting to it. Todd sent you with a message? Well if it's the same as before you can tell him, no deal."

"I don't know about before. But do you want to hear this or not? I've my pride too you know."

Karl reached out. "I'm sorry, don't mind me. Prison does things to you. Please: Deliver your message."

Gary's confidence restored, he leant forward confidentially. "Todd can get you out of prison, at a price."

"How?"

"I don't know. He didn't tell me. But I believe him, with Todd anything is possible."

Karl considered. It was the most hopeful news he'd heard in weeks. "Tell Todd I want to see him in person."

"I don't think he'll come. You know how he feels about prisons."

"I know how I feel about prisons and I'm stuck here. He came before. Tell him either he comes or there's no deal. I'm not trusting this to any go-between, not even you Gary. No offence."

"I know. But don't shoot the messenger will you?"

Karl laughed. "Where do you pick these things up from? You surprise me sometimes. Watch out for yourself. I depend on you."

"Same here. We're family aren't we? Well I'd better be off. See a man about a dog."

Karl winced. "Don't get too colourful Gary. Well, good luck."

Gary waved and was gone.

Chapter Eighteen

The weeks followed in monotonous sequence and Karl heard nothing. How could he stand ten years of this? After only weeks, he was climbing the walls. In the end he'd go crazy.

Desperate, he asked himself whether it had been a try-on by Todd, to get his hands on a fortune. Or had Gary garbled the message? For there were limits even to Todd's power and influence, and prisons were built with thick walls and several layers of security. You couldn't simply stroll out one evening.

Then suddenly a message came: Todd wanted to see him. After some negotiation with the authorities it was allowed.

Like prize fighters weighing each other up before the big bout, both men seated themselves either side of the table in the visiting room.

"You're looking pale. Prison food not agreeing with you?" Todd began slowly.

"Nothing about prison agrees with me, as well you should remember."

A slight shudder passed through Todd and he looked warily about him. "An experience I'm not anxious to repeat, I agree."

Karl lowered his voice. "So what's the deal? Can you get me out of here?"

Todd nodded. "I can fix it so that you can come and go as you please. Treat the place like a hotel if you will."

"Some hotel. Listen: I thought you had an escape plan."

"And go on the run for ever? This way is better. I've some special jobs lined up for you. Prison is the perfect alibi."

"Why should I risk my neck doing these special jobs when I could stay tucked up in here?"

"Freedom – and a share of the take. Plus, while you're out you can try and locate Judy. I'm sure she's alive somewhere, and laughing at you."

Karl had gone rigid and white, so that Todd was seriously concerned he might collapse. "Karl, Karl pull yourself together before the warders come over. We haven't long."

Karl's face twitched as he tried to come out of it. He seemed to be pulled in opposite directions of rage and relief at once. "You think she's alive and has watched me go to prison for ten years. I can't believe it. No one could do such a thing. No one could."

"Don't you believe it."

"I should have known she could be that devious."

"Of course you should. Anyway listen, time is short. I've straightened one of the screws here. Robinson. After what I have on him he'll do anything for me. He's assigned to your prison wing. He'll smuggle you out with him in screws' uniform at the end of his shift. Then back again at the start of his next. He and his pal will vouch for you that you were in your cell all the time."

Karl looked doubtful. "It sounds very iffy. What if I'm recognised?"

"But of course it's risky. Getting out of prison always is. But it's worked before – for your father. So you can trust me."

"And once I'm out, what are these special jobs?"

"Police compounds. I've cased them: they're full of confiscated drugs, copper, cars, you name it."

"Police compounds! It's asking for trouble."

Todd's face broke into a malignant smile. "Their security is poor. They never imagine they could be targets. They'll not know what hit them."

"But you've still to dispose of the stuff. You'll be red hot. There's something else behind this which you're not telling me, isn't there?"

"All right. This is war. Gloves off. They insulted me, degraded me when I was inside, and took away my profession. Now they're going to suffer. After the compounds, it's their homes. I know where they live."

Karl was appalled. Had Todd taken leave of his senses? Prison must have made him snap. "Steady on Harold. Let's not turn this into a vendetta. We'll be the losers."

"Not with your alibi. We'll humiliate them and they won't be able to do a thing about it. I'll show them who is boss."

Karl let Todd run out of steam, then started to check out some details. "How do we attack these compounds?"

"Cam ram raiders. Like I said, their security isn't what it's cracked up to be. We smash our way in."

"You mean I do. I suppose you'll be far away with your own unbreakable alibi. But never mind that. I have to decide now?"

"Well how much longer do you want to rot here, doing nothing to prove your innocence or get even with Judy who put you here."

Karl looked at those small calculating eyes, and that ugly potato head. There was a sort of indestructibility about Todd, dangerous, a little mad. But he'd make it work. He'd get Karl out of there.

"All right. I'll do it. Just make sure this Robinson is properly straightened. I don't want him marching me up to the governor's office."

"He's in my pocket. Relax. In fact Robinson will tell you when we're pulling you out."

"So I just have to sit on my hands and wait?"

Todd rose slowly and cast a baleful eye on Karl and his surroundings. "What else is there to do in a place like this?" Then he left, his great girth swaying between the rows of tables.

Chapter Nineteen

Often as he sat in his cell Karl felt he must be in shock: things kept happening to him, people like Todd told him things, but nothing seemed to sink in. Despite Todd's claims he didn't know if Judy was dead or alive, didn't know if he was a murderer or not, or what to feel and how to react. Accordingly his moods seemed to change by the hour, until he was exhausted and determined never to feel anything again.

He was slouched in a trough of despondency when the prison officer Robinson looked in furtively. "It's on for tonight." Heavy, round shouldered, Robinson wore the guilty but determined expression of a family man with nothing to gain but everything to lose. Hollow.

"What?" Karl's brain was befuddled.

"Don't act dumb and strain my patience. Your friend Todd has set it up for tonight. Here . . ." and he quickly passed a bundle of clothes to Karl, "put these on."

"What are they?"

"Prison officer's uniform, of course. How else do you think we're going to get you past everyone and outside?"

Grimly Karl jumped up and began to change. A plan was forming in his mind. He'd go along with Todd for the moment. After all, if it was getting him out of this shit hole. He was beginning to think he'd rot there for ever.

Robinson kept look-out, darting his head frequently round the door into the walkway. "For goodness sake, speed it up can't you? We don't want you found with your trousers down."

Karl tidied himself up and stashed away his own clothes under the blanket of his bed to simulate someone sleeping. "All right,

I'm ready. Now what?"

"Just walk briskly, stay close to me. Don't look anyone in the face. I'll cover you, and just appear to be in conversation with me."

Karl nodded nervously. What if he was recognised?

Robinson reassured him: "There's lots of us, and we've had some recent transfers from other prisons so if challenged I'll say you're new here."

They set off quickly down the gangway and then along a maze of corridors and stairways.

Robinson knew the most obscure route, where they were least likely to encounter other prison officers loitering in groups who might ask awkward questions.

The prison was old, built of monumental grey stone and Karl felt as if he were escaping from a fortress. Fortunately, large buttresses, fire buckets, and trolleys provided excellent cover and they slipped largely unnoticed towards the entrance.

That shift of prison officers was milling about, anxious to be off. Robinson handed Karl an overcoat and nodded for him to put it on, while he donned his own.

Then amidst some horseplay about the recent football result the prison officers marshalled themselves for a quick exit.

Karl was carried along with the crowd and suddenly he was outside being led by Robinson to follow the perimeter wall round towards the car park. The night air felt to Karl fresh and cool like submerging his head in a mountain stream. He paused, drinking it in, till Robinson urged him: "Come on, hurry it up. We don't want you discovered here at the last minute."

Pulling himself together Karl hastened to follow Robinson to his car.

Once inside Robinson muttered, "I take you to the abandoned petrol forecourt just outside town and that's me finished. I'll pick you up from there when you've done the job. Todd knows."

Karl nodded and then had to ask: "Why are you doing this?"

Robinson's mouth set in a firm, sick line. "I've no choice. Don't ever let Todd get something on you. He's like a leech, never lets go."

"So it's not for money?"

Robinson laughed bitterly. "Money? When do I ever see any money? I'll probably end up doing time myself for this lot. So just don't mess it up. That's all."

"I won't."

Together they sat in silence, as the car sped down the dark, rain splashed streets, towards the outskirts of town. Finally the derelict forecourt appeared in their headlights and Robinson pulled the car across to a halt.

Seconds later Todd appeared, head bent under a cagoule to avoid the rain. "You brought him then, good. Hop out Karl. We haven't all night."

Robinson nodded sourly. "Get him back half an hour before shift start. I don't want to be late smuggling him back in."

"Yes, all right, who's organising this show? Now get off."

Robinson muttered about danger and ingratitude, and then drove off, glad to be away from the scene of his complicity.

"Here," and Todd directed Karl over to the empty forecourt cabin. He passed a pile of clothes. "You can change in there and then give me the uniform and I'll keep it till later."

Eagerly, despite the wind howling through the empty window frames, Karl changed. It suddenly felt wonderful to be on the outside in normal, non-prison clothes.

"Now here's the plan," Todd began. "There's a police compound down Ackerley Way, past the cemetery . . ."

"Hang on a minute," Karl interrupted. "You can save your breath. I've been thinking it all over and I'm off. I may never get another chance so I'm disappearing. Thanks for getting me out Harold, but I've no intention of going back inside."

Todd's eyes narrowed and the battering rain further darkened his mood. "Oh I see. I get you out and then you double-cross me."

"I'm sorry Harold, but you've been inside, you know what it's like. I can't stand it."

Todd's bulk moved forward and he grabbed Karl's jacket front. "Well you're just going to have to stand it for a little while longer. How long do you think you'd last undetected out here without my help?"

"Take your hands off me," Karl said with a deadly quiet in his voice, and lifted Todd's hands away. "I'll take my chances. But I'm not breaking and entering for you or anybody."

"Now you listen to me. You'll do whatever I tell you to. I lifted you out of that place, and I can drop you straight back in it. And then you'll never get out. I can locate Judy for you – if she's still alive. I can deliver a pardon and any revenge you name. On my conditions. Do I make myself clear?"

Karl paused. He couldn't argue with Todd's logic. As usual this man had every angle sewn up. He made Karl feel like an amateur. "But if I get caught on one of your jobs it will only make things worse for me."

"How could they be worse? You can't locate Judy, prove she's alive and you didn't kill her, from your prison cell; without me you'll serve your full term. I don't think you understand – I'm all you've got. Take it or leave it. And make it sharp. This wind and rain is doing terrible things to my arthritis."

Suddenly Karl saw that the sodden, overblown arthritic body in front of him was his last resort. "All right Harold, you win. Police compound in Ackerley, down by the cemetery."

"That's right. I'll drop you half a mile away. There's a stolen Land-rover with reinforced bull bars on the front. Here are the keys. The compound gate is old ironwork, weak at the hinges. Just drive in at full throttle and you'll smash through. Then load up with all the movables. There should be plenty of copper, precious metals. Even some drugs."

"Drugs?"

"Now you are not going sensitive on me, are you?"

"No, all right. Only don't get me thinking too much about what I may find."

"That's right. You leave the thinking to me. What a thing to pull off, eh? Won't the police look sick. It'll be all across the newspapers in the morning."

"And they'll be good and angry and come looking for us."

Todd rubbed his fleshy hands together. "And they'll find I was miles away drinking with cronies very publicly all night, and you'll have been vouched for by Robinson, safely tucked up in prison."

"I hope so Harold. I have terrible feelings about all this."

"Just nerves lad. You're your father's son, it's in the blood. You can do it. I wouldn't have picked you else."

"Thanks a lot," replied Karl with bitter irony. The last thing he wanted was to follow in his father's criminal footsteps.

"So let's step on it. Everything clear?"

Karl nodded and Todd drove him through the darkened streets down past the park and the cemetery to the dropping-off point.

"There it is." Todd pointed and Karl could see the green Land-rover tucked in a side road and masked by a large overhanging tree.

"Now think on," urged Todd. "These police bastards have screwed you and me. This is our chance to pay them back. Smack them right where it hurts."

Karl nodded, yet not totally convinced. He walked slowly across to the Land-rover, conscious of Todd's eyes following him every inch of the way.

Just like Robinson he was caught in Todd's net. If he ever wanted a pardon, ever wanted to confront Judy and make her pay he had to go along with Todd's scheme. Todd never did anything for nothing.

So Karl started up the Land-rover and drove carefully to the compound. There it stood, a fenced-off yard with some old victorian warehouse buildings inside. Trust the police not to spend any money on it. There were big notices telling trespassers to keep out and warning dire consequences, but it was all bluff. The rust and decay told their own story.

Karl sat and bit his nail, the engine turning over ominously in the background. He must be mad, he told himself. He'd never gone in for blagging before. Selling dodgy merchandise yes, but this was entering a new league. Ever since he'd met Judy he'd been sucked into a world of heavy crime which was alien to him.

But all the time he was impelled forward. There was no going back; all of them – Judy, Todd, the police – had made sure of that. Well let it be on their heads then. He'd had enough. Maybe Todd was right: it was pay-back time. He was sick of trying to figure it all out. In the end all that mattered was action.

He let in the clutch, revved the engine, and the Land-rover catapulted towards the compound entrance. He was suddenly on a high as the vehicle picked up speed, and then he braced himself, hands firmly on the wheel. The bull bars collided head on with the old gate and buckled it, hinges awry.

Karl reversed, pulling the gate with him, then accelerated again and the buckled centre section gave, letting him through.

Suddenly he was parked in the centre of the yard, entirely visible and vulnerable. He raced out of the cab, taking a wrench and sledgehammer with him.

Then he was breaking old locks and tired splintered doors to disgorge the contents of the warehouse outbuildings. Hastily he filled sacks with everything shiny and valuable he could lay his hands on. Minutes were ticking by and he was convinced he was going to be discovered.

Dragging the now heavy sacks through the mud somehow he managed to haul them in the back of the Land-rover.

Then he told himself that it was enough. He was not risking his neck any more. That lot would have to do Todd.

Jumping back into the Land-rover he reversed round. The wheels caught in a pothole, and he had visions of being stuck, revving his wheels uselessly. But then they gripped and the vehicle lurched forward over the flattened, tangled wreck of fencing, and out through the gaping entrance.

He cried out, "I've done it!" and cheered until the dark night sobered him up, and he told himself not to blow it.

Todd was impatient at the forecourt meeting place, and couldn't wait to look in the back of the Land-rover at the haul.

"Is this all?"

"What do you mean?" Karl snarled. "I risked everything to get this for you. Here, take it before I change my mind."

"All right," Todd said ungraciously. "I suppose it will have to do. Maybe there's more here than at first meets the eye. Help me."

"Do it yourself." But to hurry things up, Karl reluctantly helped him down with the loaded sacks.

Once they were transferred to the boot of his car, Todd told Karl, "Now, I'll ditch the Land-rover. Here's your uniform, change in the cabin then wait for Robinson." He looked at his watch. "He should pick you up in about five hours."

"Five hours in that freezing hole!" Karl was appalled.

"Look, while you're out of prison and in that uniform you're hotter than hot. No one would think of checking this godforsaken spot. Just doss down on the floor of the cabin and get some sleep. I'll be back in a few minutes to pick up your clothes and my car.

With that he was off, leaving Karl cursing as he changed again with the cutting wind slicing through every crevice and broken window in the cabin.

"Damn him. Soon he'll be warm with his scotch counting the

take. And I'm stuck here in the middle of nowhere, freezing my balls off waiting for someone who may never come. Then what?"

His teeth were chattering as he sat down in a corner of the cabin and clutched his clothes round him for warmth. He found a rough piece of filthy carpet and snuggled under that.

Eventually Todd returned, but only to collect the clothes and pick up his car. Seeing Karl's woebegone figure he said, "Maybe I was a bit harsh about the haul. There was more than I thought there. Even some antique gold." His eyes glittered. "Don't worry, I'll keep your share safe. A nice little nest egg for when you come out."

From the depths of his chilled frame Karl rounded on him: "Yes, but when do I come out? I'm not doing this for ever."

"Of course not. Believe me, I am working on finding a trace of Judy every spare minute I get. As soon as I have news I'll tell you. Then you'll be pardoned and freed. Think of that."

"I'm thinking of stoving her face in, that's what I'm thinking of at this precise moment if I ever get my hands on her."

"Now you're tired and emotional. You don't want to be pardoned and then straight back inside for murder, do you?"

"Right now I don't know or care. I'd just give anything to be warm, in a proper bed without all these crazy thoughts going round my head."

Todd retreated. "Right. Well hang on. You'll be free soon," and he left his disgruntled escapee muttering and cursing to himself.

As he climbed back in his car Todd murmured, "Sometimes I wonder about that boy. If he's not cracked yet, he soon will be. And then he'll be no use. Maybe I'd better find Judy after all."

Chapter Twenty

At Todd's next meeting with Karl in prison several weeks later, he was surprised to find Karl totally distracted.

"I wish you'd concentrate," bemoaned Todd as Karl seemed to look everywhere but at him. "You can't get so many visits."

At Karl's hard look even Todd knew he'd gone too far. I'm sorry lad, I shouldn't have said that. Not the most tactful remark."

"Too right."

"Yes, well OK, but I don't see what's biting you. The raid was a great success. Boy, were the police's face red when it was plastered all over the front pages of the papers. And the haul was better than I thought at first sight. You picked up some real gems. You're a natural, with your father's instinct."

"I wish you'd leave my father out of it."

There was another tense silence.

"Well come on Karl, out with it. I thought you'd be pleased: one in the eye for them, eh?"

"Yes but I'm still stuck in here aren't I?" snarled Karl. "That's what's up with me. This place," and he waved his arm around, till a screw's disapproving gaze dissuaded him. "Look: I can't even wave my arm without someone putting the block on. I tell you I feel sometimes I'm going mad in here, no one to talk to, nothing to do."

"No one to talk to?"

"I know the place is full to bursting. But I've nothing in common with them. And no female company."

"Ah," Todd sighed significantly. He wished he could have had a fraction of Karl's women in the past, but knew this would be no consolation to Karl now. "I know it's tough son. I've been inside too."

"Yes, but you've not been used to getting as much," Karl taunted him callously. "Me, I can't do without it. It's been too long."

Todd spread his arms helplessly. He didn't know what he could say, and resented Karl's cruel jibe.

Karl leant forward and lowered his voice. "Next time you get me out I want Sarah, understand me? Fix it."

Todd's potato face began to sweat, and jerked evasively. "How can I? You'll blow the perfect alibi, everything. A few more jobs and we'll be set for life. Just be patient."

"I've been nothing but, now no more. I want Sarah. She'll understand. I must have her or I'll go out of my tree."

Todd spread out anxious fingers to calm Karl down. "All right. Don't draw attention to yourself. I'll see what I can do. But what if she won't see you? She thinks you killed her sister."

Karl's face was ravaged, anguished. "She can't still think that. She knows me too well. Talk to her, convince her. You know I wouldn't kill Judy."

Todd looked evasive, doubtful. "Well not intentionally. But she's not popped up either, dead or alive. It's a real puzzle, I have to say."

"Hey, who's side are you on?" Karl rounded on him. I thought you were working on finding her. If you've been double-crossing me, I'll have your guts for garters."

"Of course I've been trying. I just haven't had any luck. I simply meant I can't guarantee Sarah's feelings – or a warm place for you in her bed which is what you want, isn't it?"

Karl nodded miserably, desperate. "She loves me, I know she does," he murmured. "Ever since I told her it was she and not Judy I should have married."

"But if she thinks you killed Judy to be with her . . ?"

"But that's crazy. No one would think they could get away with a thing like that."

"Well the jury were convinced, weren't they? Dark night, secluded wood. Everyone gone: no one to witness a murder."

"Yes I know what they all said. But it doesn't make sense and Sarah must see that. Talk to her, won't you?"

"I'll do my best."

"You'd better not fail me Todd, or there'll be no more ram

96

raids."

Todd's face went stony, his fists clenched. "Now don't threaten me sonny boy. I'm an old hand. It works both ways. Do you want me to leave you here, sit it out for the rest of your sentence?"

"No, but you need me too."

"My point exactly. We need each other. I get you out, you do the raids, and we'll fix you up with a bit of nooky. What do you say?"

"Nooky indeed. It has to be Sarah. Don't try and fix me up with some tart because it won't wash."

"As if I would. All right, I'll work on Sarah and let you know. But be ready for the next job, whatever. No backing out when Robinson gives you the nod, or the whole deal's off, including Sarah."

"All right." Karl was subdued. The waiting to see Sarah would be terrible.

"By the way, how's Robinson been?"

Surprised, Karl responded: "Fine. He was a bit cool on return and wouldn't hear anything about the job, but that's good really isn't it? What have you got on him?"

"Never you mind. Just be grateful."

"Is there anybody in this town you haven't fixed?"

Todd smiled. "Not that I can think of, off hand. Knowing where the bodies are buried, that's the secret in this life." Then at Karl's pointed look: "No offence meant. Just a figure of speech. Besides you keep assuring me Judy's not buried anywhere, don't you?"

"That's right and I'll keep on till somebody believes me."

"Or till you've convinced yourself."

"You're an evil bastard sometimes Harold."

"It's part of my deadly charm. Think about it. I don't care whether you killed her or not. In fact, if you had you would be more use to me."

"Well I can't oblige."

"No? Well we'll see. Goodbye. Keep your pecker up. Oh you're doing that anyway, aren't you?"

"Get lost, you vulgar . . ."

"Lost for words? Well you'll have plenty of time to think of a reply, for when we meet again."

Karl was rising to his feet, his anger building dangerously.

e

"Get out of my sight, before I stick one on you."

But Todd could be surprisingly quick on his feet, and was gone.

Todd set off on his errand to Sarah. She always made him feel uncomfortable, with that aloof way of hers towards him as if he had just crawled out from under a stone. What was her secret? How did she come by that immense self-possession, that ice-maiden quality?

She frustrated him: he had nothing on her, no guilty secret with which to blackmail or humble her. And that angered him, forced him to submit to her high-handed rejection of him.

There she stood, tending seed boxes in her greenhouse. She wore a baggy Scandinavian jumper, sleeves rolled up, jeans and trainers, but still contrived to be sensual and alluring. Her brown rounded arms weaved among the trays, while her curvaceous back leant over the seedlings tenderly. Her shiny hair was tied back and her oval face bore one of her characteristic meditative looks, long lashes over those hazel eyes.

"Sarah," he called, mustering his normal authority, and waddled across to her.

Sarah looked up, taken by surprise, then her mouth set in distaste as she saw who was approaching. She had never known any good to come from an encounter with Harold Todd.

"Good afternoon," she answered politely and then continued with the seed boxes.

"Can I speak to you for a minute?"

"Certainly," but her head remained lowered avoiding eye contact.

"Oh for heaven's sake, stop prodding those bits of stalks and listen. I've come from Karl."

Sarah paused and raised her face to look at him. "So?" she said coldly.

"He's desperate, missing you."

"Well he shouldn't have killed my sister, should he? The nerve of the man."

"You don't really believe that?"

Sarah became uncomfortable, shifting her weight onto the other foot. "Why not? There's been no trace of her since."

"Lots of people disappear without being dead. She could have engineered it."

"Why should she? She went up into those hills because she was crazy about him. I know."

Todd's face couldn't disguise his distaste for her naïvety. "Come off it. They fought like cat and dog – mostly over you."

"Me?"

"Yes, Karl told me all about his confession of love for you, and the carrying on behind Judy's back."

Sarah's face glowed in anger and humiliation. "He told you that? Good God." And her hands clenched and unclenched. Then she forced herself to be calm. "Yes, it's true. We couldn't help ourselves."

"A fine pair."

"Yes, all right. I'm not proud of it."

"So – about Judy?"

"I don't know. When you've been as close as us – well it's been hell, losing her, not knowing. Sometimes I think I have a sister's instinct that she's alive. And then it fades and I think I'm deluding myself. After all, she would have given me a sign, something to let me know if she was alive."

"Not if she was punishing you both, or if the risk were too great."

Sarah gazed at him amazed, incredulous. "This is my sister, my own flesh and blood we're talking about. However we might have fallen out over a man, she'd never do that to me. She wouldn't put me through this."

Todd's superior smile broadened. "Not just a man, remember, but her husband. That changes a woman, believe me. Every other woman becomes an enemy, a competitor. And you had destroyed her self-belief by proving that Karl preferred you."

Sarah was nodding, automatically trying to adjust to this new theory of events.

"Anyway, to get back to my errand, Karl wants to see you again."

"I couldn't. Come to the prison to visit my sister's killer?"

Secretly Todd despised her. "You don't have to. I can get Karl out, just for a night. He'll come to you."

"For a night?" Sarah quietly echoed. "You mean?"

"He's been banged up for months with no woman. He wants

99

you. He's going crazy."

Despite herself Sarah's heart suddenly went out to him, but then recoiled. "Well fix him up with a tart if that's all he wants."

"I haven't time to listen to this. I'll bring him to the flat at ten tonight. Don't disappoint him."

"Tonight? I need time to think. I don't know what I feel."

"Ten tonight and that's final. You can sort out your scruples in the meantime."

He turned to go, tired of Sarah's sensibilities.

"But stop. How can you get him out tonight? Have you keys to the prison or something?"

"As good as. Karl is doing a service for me in return."

"I might have known. Well I'm not promising. Karl may find an empty flat."

Todd shook his head. "Don't give me that. You'll be there. You're gagging for it."

"You scum. Go away and tell Karl I never want to see him again."

"Well," Todd smiled. "A little fire at last. The ice maiden melts. Look me up when you've had enough of young Casanova."

"Get lost."

"I'm going," and Todd walked away, pleased at least to have broken through her cold reserve, and made her heart beat faster. He had her measure now.

Chapter Twenty-one

It was approaching midnight when Karl apprehensively knocked on the door of the flat. He had his jacket collar pulled up and was edgy, on the balls of his feet, ready to run if this was a set up. But after a couple of tense minutes waiting, the door opened an inch and Sarah peered out at him.

"You've got a nerve," she hissed. "Why don't you go away and leave me alone?"

"Sarah, let me in. I'm freezing out here and anyone might see me." He pushed on the door and with a reluctant cry Sarah fell back.

"How dare you come barging in here?"

"Oh come off it Sarah you were expecting me or you wouldn't be here."

"I happen to live here now. I moved back in after, after . . ." she found it impossible to say the words.

"After Judy disappeared," Karl completed for her.

Then he strode forward and took Sarah's gentle, oval face in his hands. "I didn't kill her you know. I've never killed anyone. I couldn't, wouldn't."

Sarah gazed at him, bewildered, hot tears forcing themselves out. "Oh Karl, what am I supposed to think? You had a fight in the woods didn't you?"

"Yes, but she only tumbled down an earth work. I thought she'd walked away with a few bruises."

"But you don't know, she could have fractured her skull down there. Or did you go down and finish her off with that scythe they found?"

Karl pulled back from her. "Not you too? I thought you at least

101

would understand. Judy flew at me like a wild animal. I had my share of cuts and bruises too."

"You poor injured soul," Sarah told him sarcastically. "Why didn't you go down and make sure she was all right?"

"Maybe I should have done. But she would have only torn into me again. And the point is: if I killed her she'd have still been down there. But obviously she got up and walked away."

"So you say."

"Look, will you try and understand and have faith in me, or not? Because otherwise I'm going."

"Go on, see if I care."

Then as Karl retreated to the door, Sarah relented: "No Karl, I can't do it. Don't go. I believe you. Judy is as tough as they come. She's alive somewhere, glorying in all that she's putting us through."

Karl came forward, eyes widening. "So you think it's a put up job?"

Sarah looked down. "I hate to say it about my own sister but it looks like it. I keep having this feeling that she's somewhere near and that she knows what I'm thinking. It sends shivers down my spine. I know it sounds crazy but when you've been as close as Judy and I, like twins . . ."

Karl held her close. "I'm glad you feel it too, because it gives me hope."

And he kissed her, hard passionate kisses on the lips, and Sarah wrapped her arms around him. And then he half carried her through to the bedroom and began pulling off her clothes.

"Don't tear them," Sarah appealed to him, but seeing his eyes said: "Oh do what you want. Take me, I'm all yours."

Karl pushed her back on top of the bed and quickly undressed himself. Then he thrust himself upon her.

"Please slow down. More gently," she coaxed him. "I know it's been a long time."

Karl tried not to rush her but his desire was immense and impatient. Sarah stroked his hair and wound herself around him.

He cried out in passion and ecstasy and she smiled serenely at giving so much pleasure. Her own would come.

Then the bedroom door opened and a figure was silhouetted in the space.

Karl put his arm up to shade his eyes and protect himself.

"Judy?"

Then he was diving off the bed in case a gunshot or knife was heading his way.

Sarah lay bewildered, not knowing what was going on. "Who is it? Is it you Judy?"

The figure grinned. "You two want your eyes testing. Sorry to spoil your fun but I've waited as long as I could. You left the front door open."

Karl knelt up from the floor rubbing his eyes in disbelief. "Dad? Is that your voice? It can't be, you're dead."

"If I am I'm doing a very good impersonation of walking about."

Slowly Karl rose to his feet and then grabbed some clothes to cover his nakedness.

Sarah slid further under the bedclothes in fear, embarrassment, and humiliation. "You might have knocked," she croaked.

"I am very sorry, you're quite right. You must be Sarah. Pleased to meet you."

Sarah nodded and motioned to Karl to pass her clothes.

Karl did so. Then dressing, followed his father out to the lounge.

"Very nice," his father commented. "Very nice indeed. I like that," he said, pointing to an Art Nouveau print.

"Dad, what is all this? Where did you pop up from?"

"Well not from the grave, that's for sure. Shall we sit down?"

Sarah took her usual chair, and Karl and his father sat opposite each other.

Frank seemed to Karl frailer than before, but was still a large, rangy man, all muscle and bone. He had a hard squarish face and a spare patch of tightly razored grey hair. He wore an old check suit.

"I suppose Todd put you on to us," Karl took up a resigned voice.

"Who else? He's my only contact. But not the nicest or most trustworthy of men."

Involuntarily Karl shuddered. "No. But listen: you were reported dead."

"A man with the same name was released from prison about the same time. He died soon afterwards and the newspapers got their wires crossed and put my photo on the obituary. So I decided to stay dead for a while."

Karl looked his father straight in the eye with a dangerous warning gaze. "Why?" The note was ominous.

"Not to cause you any bother I swear it. I want to help. I know you never murdered this Judy. Whatever I can do, just ask. I want to make a new start with you."

"A new start! Don't make me laugh."

Sarah reached out towards Karl. "Don't. Let your father speak."

Karl rounded on her cruelly. "Shut up, and don't interfere when you know nothing about it. For your information this man ruined my life. He was the worst father a man could have."

"Karl!" Sarah burst out horrified.

"Hey now, steady on," Frank rejoined.

"Have you forgotten the children's homes and you turning up drunk?"

Frank dropped his head to reveal a now scrawny neck. "No, you're right, I was a lousy father." He turned to Sarah: "You see me and his mother split up when he was just a lad, and she buggered off. Well I couldn't cope."

He caught Karl's eye. "Well I suppose I didn't try very hard. Men didn't bring up kids on their own in those days."

"So he stuck me in one children's home after another. Then in a rush of guilt he'd sweep me up and take me on a binge to London. We'd swan around with all his gangster friends, and Dad would get plastered. I'd be hanging around hotel rooms waiting for him to sober up. And then he'd drop me like a stone, back in the children's home. Have you any idea what that felt like?"

Frank's eyes were misty. "I'm sorry son, truly I am. I never meant to hurt you. I wanted us to be close, like a father and son ought to be. But it wasn't meant."

"Oh but you tried, didn't you Dad, fixing me up in the family firm?" He turned to Sarah. "Every time I visited him in prison, later on, it was the same story: he had this great job lined up for when he got out and I must help him."

"So you stopped visiting," his father spoke bitterly.

"Do you blame me? Think what a shining example I had in front of me. I didn't want to end up like you. Now look at me."

"Ah fair dos. I was quite a man in those days. Much respected. Well known. Even the Krays listened to me."

"You're living in fairy-tale land. No one respected you. You were just a berk of a burglar who got caught too often."

"I wasn't – I was a big man."

"No you weren't."

There was a long silence while Frank wrung his hands in awkwardness. "I didn't want our reunion to go like this, raking over old ground, with so much bitterness. Can't we put the past behind us?"

Karl gave him an anguished look. "How can we? You're old crony Todd is still crawling all over me. But he's the only one who can get me out of prison, like this."

"I know, and I came to warn you against Todd. Don't do any jobs for him. He's bad news. I should know. Let me help you instead."

"Listen to you. You're a fine one to talk, warning me off Todd. Can you get me out of prison?"

"I don't know. But say we'll meet up again and you'll think about what I've said. Don't shut me out of your life. I couldn't bear it. You're all I have left."

"Don't Dad, don't play on my sympathies. I don't know."

Frank grasped at that eagerly. "You won't regret it. And I'm changed. I won't let you down this time. I promise."

"Please Dad, don't promise."

"All right son, I won't."

Frank rose, bade a polite farewell to Sarah and then insisted on hugging Karl before sliding out into the night.

Karl watched him go and then turned to Sarah and whistled. "Where did the old bugger spring from? He always could work the ring on me. Well not this time, I've had enough."

"But Karl, look at him."

"I was. But, you see, I know him of old. Don't be taken in. He'll never change. He's only jealous of Todd muscling in. You'll see, he'll come back to cut me in on one last big job of his own. Well he's out of luck."

"I hope so," Sarah echoed. "Now can we go back to bed."

"I can't, I've a . . . job on."

"Oh Karl. Listen to yourself. Well then I wash my hands of you. Your father was right. Go on. You're well suited, the two of you." And Sarah slammed the bedroom door behind her.

Chapter Twenty-two

"Tom, there's someone out there, watching the house. I can feel it."

"Nonsense Judy, get a grip on yourself. It's being couped here, that's all."

"Thanks a bunch for your support." Judy prowled up and down the living-room, keeping out of sight of the windows.

"For goodness sake don't get careless now. Stay out of sight!" Randle warned her.

"I am. Stop treating me like a child. I could scream." She cast a hard, distraught face to the ceiling. "How did I get into this mess?"

Ruffled, Randle strode across to confront her. "You wanted it, remember? Karl put away and you out of the frame."

Judy sighed. She wondered now if it had been so important to be free of Karl, even with his infidelity. Bitterly she reminded herself that she was in an even smaller prison than Karl, because she couldn't stray beyond four walls.

Randle's home was hardly palatial: it was as old, tired, and threadbare as he was. A '30s semi without grace or charm, wearing a squat witches'-hat roof. The decor was floral wallpaper, stick furniture, and a sagging three-piece suite with scorched wooden arms.

Then Judy came back to the present: "Will you check?"

"What?"

"I tell you someone's out there."

Wearily Randle sloped upstairs and from behind a curtain, checked the street in both directions. There was the odd passerby, but he could see no one suspicious. Angry at his wasted time, he let the curtain drop back and clambered back downstairs again.

"I can't see anyone. It must be your imagination."

"Stop patronising me. I tell you someone was out there. It's spooky. I can't stay here for ever. It's like a tomb, buried alive," and she shivered, rubbing her arms round herself.

"Don't let go now. Just a little longer, and I can sell up and we can go to live in the sun."

Judy grabbed him by the arm. "Yes, but how much longer do we have to wait? I warn you I can't stand it, doing nothing. Seeing nobody. I'm not used to it."

"You've got me."

There was a pause. "Yes, I've got you."

"Don't sound too enthusiastic will you? But remember we're in this together. I'm going to live it up, with you on my arm."

"I'm not some damn fashion accessory."

"Don't swear. You'll be whatever I want you to be. I've waited a lifetime for this and you're not screwing it up."

"Or else?"

"Oh use your head. Without me you have no future – unless you fancy prison."

Judy scowled. "Would there be a difference?"

Randle was like a leech, and she couldn't shake him off. He'd stick with her to the ends of the earth. She told herself to bide her time till they'd moved away together, then she could just disappear. But what if she couldn't? He'd find her. Then her only way out would be to kill him. Or maybe he'd kill her to stop her ever leaving him.

She had to talk to somebody or she'd go out of her mind. Inexorably she was being drawn back to Sarah. They shared a strange telepathy. As kids they'd even had their own secret language. She couldn't bear to be cut off from Sarah. Sarah was her better angel, keeping her from harm.

Accordingly, later the next day when Randle was out, Judy sneaked away from the house.

From the vantage point of a pedestrian overbridge she could see Sarah, absorbed in tending her plants in the greenhouses. She was as graceful as ever, even in her rolled-up Fair Isle sweater and long green peasant skirt. Judy felt a fierce pang at all the anger and jealousy that had passed between them over Karl. If only there was some way of resolving it.

Judy walked quickly down from the bridge and skirted the main road, keeping to back streets and the protection of high scrub along wasteland and allotments leading to the greenhouses.

She waited, nerves tautened by this, her first expedition from Randle's house. What a risk she was taking. If someone spotted her the whole scheme was blown sky high.

How would Sarah react? If she went straight to the police that would finish Judy, too. But she knew that Sarah would never do that to her. They were too close, weren't they?

From behind the comparative seclusion of a small garden shed Judy called out, low, "Sarah."

Sarah stopped, fingers at the roots of a pot plant, as if frozen. Then slowly, dazed, she turned around.

Judy signalled urgently to her not to speak but to join her behind the shed where they couldn't be seen from the road.

Slowly, mechanically Sarah replaced the pot on the tray and walked across. Judy, alive, after thinking she might never see her again. Sarah held Judy tightly, and they hugged each other.

"I can't believe it. I sensed something. I daren't hope but . . ."

"I'm sorry, Sarah. I never meant to put you through all that. I've been such a fool."

"Where have you been?"

"Lying low in Randle's house. I've not been outside those four walls for months. Not till now. You won't give me away, will you? I can trust you."

Sarah stiffened and pulled back. "What happened between you and Randle?"

"He's fixated on me. Sometimes I think he'd kill me if I tried to run out on him. He thinks he's sacrificed his life to save me."

"Didn't he?"

"I know, but I wasn't thinking straight. I don't want Karl to languish in prison for the rest of his life."

"So what are you going to do? Give yourself up."

Judy shook her head vehemently. "I'm not that good. I know you would, but I can't. No, I just need to get away from Randle, and then you could tell everyone it was all a terrible mistake and that I'm alive. I had amnesia or something."

"Me? You're not dragging me into all this. I see it all now. You just came to use me."

"No, it wasn't like that. I couldn't bear being separated from you for ever. If only Karl hadn't come between us."

Sarah hesitated and then told her, "I've seen Karl."

"You visited him? How is he?"

"No, he visited me, in the flat."

"What, I don't understand? How?"

"Todd has fixed one of the screws to get Karl out and in."

"Out and in again? You mean he goes back?"

Sarah nodded, while Judy clapped her hand to her head. She never would understand men.

Then Judy saw red: "You've slept with him again in the flat!"

"We thought you were dead."

"No you didn't – not really. Anyway, what about before?"

"All right, Judy, I feel guilty. The point is, Karl can get out. If he finds you he'll tear you limb from limb."

"I know. That's why I must escape, disappear before Karl is freed properly. You must keep me posted. Here's my address and phone number."

"All right. If I can I'll calm Karl down. But he's a terrible hot head."

Judy pictured Karl, and suddenly ached for him. "I did love him. But let's not get into all that again. I don't want to fight with you over him. I don't suppose I'll ever see him again."

Sarah wasn't so sure, nor of what would happen if Judy and Karl were reunited. Love or death – both seemed equally possible.

Judy began to get nervous. "I'd better go." Impulsively she hugged Sarah again, then pulled herself away. She added petulantly: "It's all Randle's fault, you know. It was his idea. He hates Karl."

Sarah nodded, wanting Judy to go now. Judy's anxiety was contagious.

"You won't let me down?" Judy stared hard at Sarah then turned and ran for cover.

Sarah shook her head at herself in disbelief. "What have I promised?"

Chapter Twenty-three

Gloria sailed down the aisles of the visiting-room like a galleon, her loose-fitting black fur coat billowing out behind her. She caught Karl's eye and fiercely pulled forward a seat to sit down as close to his face as possible. "How could you?" she hissed.

"What?"

"With Sarah. That really hurts."

Karl's face darkened. "Whose been talking?"

"It was written all over her face after your visit. Sort of lit up – which is so unusual for her. Normally she's so damn precious and refined."

She paused for breath while Karl listened perplexed and impatient. "Why did it have to be her?" She reached out for his hand and grasped it hard. "Especially after what we have?"

"Had, Gloria. It's over. But please don't broadcast it – about me and Sarah."

Gloria looked stern. "Don't panic, no one else knows. I won't tell."

"Thank God. If I'm found out I could rot in here for years."

"That's why I've come," Gloria took up eagerly. "Look," and she opened her handbag.

Karl peered over the table into it. The inside was stuffed with bank notes. "There's enough there to go anywhere together. Just say the word and you could walk out of here one bright night and never go back."

Karl was touched and embarrassed. "I don't know what to say."

Quickly Gloria intervened. "You must see I'm right. It's the only way."

But Karl wouldn't be silenced. "Gloria, I can't. I have to wait. If Todd locates Judy, I can prove my innocence and pay her back."

"Supposing Todd can't. You could be waiting in here for ever. Go away with me."

"There's no love lost between you and Judy, is there? Can't stand the competition? Judy's too like you, that's the trouble."

"Nonsense!"

"But anyway, I feel she's alive, gloating over me and Sarah."

Gloria turned away. "You disgust me, you really do. How many women do you need? You've been through this family like a dose of salts. I ought to wish well rid of you. But I can't."

"You and I were finished well before I took up with Judy."

"No we weren't. She trapped you."

"Listen: I have to see it through to the end with her."

"But why? She's been nothing but trouble for you. It could be so good again between us. Look, the money's here, waiting."

"Gloria, stop trying to buy me. I won't live off you. Put your money away."

Gloria snapped shut the catch of her handbag. "Oh get off your high horse. You've not earned a decent day's pay since you came back from London, so less of it."

Angry, Karl rose to go. Gloria looked up at him imploringly and slowly he sat down again.

"I'm sorry, I shouldn't have said that. But you keep throwing everything back in my face when all I want to do is be with you." She paused and wiped her face with her handkerchief. "If I help Todd find Judy and give her to the police, will you go away with me afterwards – when you're free?"

"You'd do that to your own daughter?"

"For you, yes."

"No promises."

"Yes, promise, I want you with me. And I won't take no for an answer."

Karl looked quizzically at her. "Then there's no point in me saying it, is there?"

Puzzled, unsure how to take this, Gloria put on a brave face and laughed. "That's right, there isn't. Oh, one last thing."

"Yes?"

"The next time you're out, visiting, I expect it to be me not

Sarah. Otherwise, all bets are off. Do I make myself clear?"

"Oh, as crystal Gloria, as always."

"Well don't try and double-cross me with her. I won't stand for it."

Gathering her fur coat around her, she rose with all the dignity she could muster and flounced out. One of the other inmates blew a raspberry and asked Karl, "What's your mother doing here again?"

Karl shrugged his shoulders: "Beats me. Must be my winning ways. She can't keep away."

Gloria was for or against you, and quite unstoppable he thought to himself. Besides, he needed all the help he could get.

Chapter Twenty-four

Karl felt damned angry: here he was out again, itchy in civilian clothes borrowed from Robinson the screw, at that same desolate abandoned petrol station. Why wasn't he hitting the city lights instead of this wrecked landscape? He was free and he should be enjoying himself, not taking on another job for Todd. It made him wonder whether it was worth being outside for just one night. Maybe Gloria had been right and he should cut and run – and keep on running. But no, he had things to do first.

Suddenly headlamps cut through the darkness and tyres crunched to a halt. A figure jumped out but Karl, dazzled by the headlights, couldn't make it out.

"Who is it?" His hands shielded his eyes from the glare.

"My but you're jumpy," came back Todd's voice.

Karl dropped his hands. "Oh it's you, at long last."

"Now don't get impatient." Todd was opposite him now. He had on a big flapping gaberdine coat and bulging wellingtons.

"So what's the job? I hope it's the last."

"What's your hurry. You're safe as houses tucked up where you are. Cast iron alibi."

"It's easy for you to talk. You should remember what it's like," he added viciously.

"All right. Now, there's been a change of plan."

"Oh?" Karl was instantly suspicious.

"Yes, the job I had in mind is scrubbed. I've something much more outstanding in view. People will never forget it."

"Get on then. I suppose it's riskier?"

"Riskier? Depends on how you look at it." Todd was enjoying himself being mysterious, tantalising.

"Look, I'm getting damned cold standing around in this hole. What is it?"

Todd grabbed him by the arm. "The chance of a lifetime to show those police high-ups that they can be paid back, destroyed for what they did to you and me."

"What are you going on about?"

"The Chief Constable is holding a special shindig at his home. Celebrating twenty years service or some such nonsense. All his senior colleagues will be there, and the top brass from other forces. It will be quite a party."

"So? Am I supposed to cheer?"

"No, you're going to destroy it."

"What? Are you mad?"

"Couldn't be saner. They won't be expecting any trouble, kalied in fact. You know how these policemen drink. So you drive right up, smash in the front door, lob in some tear gas grenades and then beat it."

Karl's jaw had dropped. Todd's mad schemes seemed to have careered out of control. "It's lunatic," he spluttered.

"No it's not. You've got this ram raiding down to a fine art. You'll have the advantage of surprise. They won't know what hit them. Think of it – all across the front pages 'Police Chiefs devastated'. That'll show them. Fame for ever."

"Twenty more years in jail like. I won't do it. I can't do it – me against that lot. Never."

"I wouldn't expect you to pull it off single-handed." Suddenly Todd was unctuous. "No, I've brought you help." He signalled and another figure jumped down out of the vehicle and walked forward in the headlights.

"Who the hell is this you've saddled me with?" Again, Karl was shielding his eyes.

"Now is that any way to talk to your half-brother?"

Karl peered harder. "Gary? Is that you? It can't be. Todd, what are you up to?"

"I couldn't lend you just anyone, could I? You want someone you can trust. And someone with muscle."

"I wanted to come," chimed in Gary. "I won't let you down. You and me – what a team, eh?"

Gary was barely recognisable: body building had swelled him inordinately.

Karl was shocked, then touched and embarrassed but bitterly angry with Todd. He pulled him to one side. "Todd, I could kill you for this. Look at him: pumped full of steroids. And what's the meaning of dragging Gary into this? He has no alibi. If anything happened to him, I'd never forgive myself, or you."

"Well who else do you suggest?" said Todd testily. "You've said yourself it's a two-man operation. Gary is all the muscle you need, and totally loyal, would do anything for you. What more could you ask?"

"I won't make use of Gary." Karl's voice rose in pain and anguish: "Look at him. You should never have let him do this to himself. You know how gullible and impressionable he is, and you trade on it."

"Oh stop being so sentimental. He wants to go doesn't he?"

Gary was feeling left out of it. "Please don't argue over me," he called to them, "I'll be all right."

"See!" Karl rounded on Todd in exasperation. "I'm at the end of my tether with you. I won't do it. Find yourself another fool."

"Trade then: do it and I'll give you Judy's address."

"She's alive!" and Karl grabbed Todd's neck, throttling him. "Where is she?"

Todd hauled himself free. "Control yourself. I'll tell you. But do this job or you'll never get to her."

"All right, anything. Where is she?"

"She's hiding out in Randle's house. I had my suspicions but she never left the house – except once, and we had her. Photograph and all. Silly girl."

"So what's the address?"

Todd scribbled it down and Karl snatched the paper off him. His eyes seemed to bore into the paper. "At last. I've got her. And she doesn't know what's coming to her." His eyes went moist then hard again. He was almost hysterical, beside himself. He began to sway.

"Hey, get a grip on yourself. You'll be fit for nothing. Gary, come over here, I want to explain tonight's operation to the two of you."

Todd went over it again in more detail and finished with: "Remember this is war and the police are the enemy."

Karl shook his head, but said nothing. Todd was power mad. Then, with a hard disbelieving stare Karl led the way to the vehicle for the drop off.

Half-an-hour later Karl and Gary were sitting in the cab of a stolen Land-rover with bull bars, waiting while Todd established an alibi for himself at a local hostelry.

Karl couldn't concentrate. Judy was alive and he had the proof! The relief almost made him want to weep. Then exhilaration shook him.

"She's alive, so I'll be free," he exclaimed and Gary willingly took his hand.

Then Karl became grave again. "Gary, you shouldn't be here, in on this. You get off while there's still time. I'll manage."

"Let you down now when you need me? No chance. I'm sticking right here." Gary seemed hyped up, unable to sit still.

"Don't be a fool. This isn't fantasy time. No bug-eyed monsters. Now go. I'm telling you to."

"No you're not. We're not kids any more. You can't order me about. I can make up my own mind and I'm staying."

"Well be it on your own head. Come on, let's give those police snobs some of their own medicine!" And he let in the clutch and the engine roared.

The Chief Constable's house was set in its own grounds, reached by a winding drive over-arched with ancient oaks and elms. It was a mock rural retreat, complete with a wishing-well and lily pond. The house was neo-georgian, an imposing red brick edifice, with mullioned windows, and a pillared portico leading to the studded front door.

Karl was all keyed up for action now as he drove quickly along the drive. Angrily he watched through the lit up downstairs windows the crush of senior policemen in their best uniforms, resplendent in braid, quaffing champagne and talking in high excited voices. All that mutual congratulation. Well he'd soon wipe the smiles off their faces.

He looked beside him: Gary's face wore a strange expression as if bewitched. "Hey, look lively. Get those grenades."

Gary pulled himself together, and reached behind his seat.

Karl was accelerating now and his pulse began to race. It was happening: victory over those stuffed shirts. Paying them back; making his mark.

The Land-rover was bouncing along now and Karl was guiding on a trajectory between those two sets of pillars in the portico. Were they wide enough? He sweated and his hands almost slipped on the wheel.

Frantically he looked and looked again, trying to judge the space. It could go either way.

The vehicle rushed forward and he was committed, too late to stop. The Land-rover thundered up the flat steps, scraped the pillars, and smashed the front door, so that the whole jamb was splintered and down like firewood.

Amidst the dust and debris Karl yelled to Gary, "Throw the grenades!" Gary reached into the box and pulled out several of the grenades which he then hurled forward out of the window.

Karl cheered at the explosions, wild with exhilaration, and then turned to one side to congratulate Gary. But Gary was pitched forward over his seat belt. His face was convulsed, and his chest was heaving like a piston. Karl thought he must be having a stroke.

In the vestibule a mob of policemen were advancing, choking, towards the vehicle. Frantically Karl threw the Land-rover into reverse and with a screeching of tyres and wrenching of gear box, the Land-rover pulled back amidst more explosions and collapsing masonry.

Karl had the Land-rover turned round now and was desperately accelerating up the drive. Gary was sprawled next to him, mad eyes staring, body contorted. Behind them, spilling out over the wreckage rushed some uniformed men, eyes streaming, angry, waving their fists and cursing.

Karl was crying. Gary needed a doctor and he'd lost his bearings. Todd was a doctor – struck off – a doctor nevertheless, he'd do something for Gary. Trying to remember the way back, Karl swore at himself for taking wrong turnings but couldn't think straight. Gary in this state: why? He'd been so hyped up for action. Just the man he needed, Todd had said. Now look at him. It was a terrible pathetic irony. Gary couldn't even help himself – mind, he never could.

It seemed to take for ever but eventually Karl made it to the meeting point. He jumped out and collared Todd. "Gary's had a seizure. Do something for him, before it's too late."

"How did it go?"

"What?"

"The Chief Constable's bash."

"Later, you idiot. See to Gary."

"All right, all right."

Todd hurried over with him and opened the door to the Land-rover. He stepped up and examined Gary and then down again.

He turned to Karl. "He's dead."

"What? He can't be. You said he was fighting fit for tonight. Otherwise he'd never have come."

"He's dead Karl. A stroke. His system just packed in."

"No, do something. Artificial respiration. Get back in there. Gary needs you."

"It's no use Karl. He's dead."

Then Karl came at him with his fists. "It's you, feeding him all those steroids, turning him into a bloated wreck like you."

Todd fended him off with his tough forearms. "Is it my fault he ate steroids like sweets? I warned him."

"You did this. I'll never forgive you."

"Look, his system just couldn't take the strain. That wasn't my fault. Now you'd better change and scarper. Leave Gary to me."

Tears forced themselves out on Karl's face. "You callous bastard. I should have taken care of him."

"Do you want me to look after things or not?"

Reluctantly Karl gave in, and got changed. Back to prison, leaving a dead brother behind. This wasn't how the evening was supposed to end.

"You do things right by Gary. Give him the best. Damn it, he had precious little of that in life," Karl called back as he was driven away by Robinson the screw.

Reverently he whispered, "Goodbye bug-eyed monster."

"You what?"

"Never mind, it doesn't matter. You wouldn't understand."

Chapter Twenty-five

Karl was given permission to attend the funeral of his half-brother. All the way to the graveyard he sat between two screws in the prison van, going over and over in his mind Gary's death.

It should never have happened. But all through their growing up they'd been separated: Karl in children's homes, Gary with his feckless mother. Frank had been a useless father to both of them. By the time they were grown up it was too late: neither could save the other.

Gary had been so guileless, so openly affectionate, shy and funny with his bug-eyed monster impressions. But he was easily hurt, sensitive over his facial appearance and puny frame. The body building had given him confidence, hope, so cruelly shattered by the steroids.

Todd had been right for once: Gary had swallowed them like sweets, ignorant of their dangers. Karl had known things were wrong, from odd comments by Gary about hearing strange voices, and his ballooning frame, obscene by the end. But what had he done about it? Nothing. And from prison what could he do?

But Todd could have, and should have prevented this. He'd have a few words for Todd at the graveside.

The church was a blackened gothic hangover from the past, surrounded by unkempt overgrown gravestones, adjacent to the sprawl of terraced streets and pubs. The van sped through the gates and Karl could see people going to the church. "If we're late I'll swing for you," Karl told the screws.

But they simply scowled and led him quickly to catch up the rear of the mourners.

The service was perfunctory. The minister had not known Gary and could only make token general condolences. Soon they were all filing out again to watch the burial.

Karl pulled away from his guards and snarled, "All right, give me space. I want to mourn my brother."

Reluctantly the screws fell back to one side, leaving Karl alone.

"I hate myself for this," Karl spoke down to the coffin. "It's so horrible. I hope you've gone to a better place."

The minister declaimed sonorously over the grave as the mourners stood around it. Afterwards Todd came and shook Karl's hand.

"I'm sorry lad, we all are. It's terrible, a young man like him."

Karl flushed. "Save your phoney pity. You're relieved you're rid of him. He was a liability wasn't he?"

"Hey, there's no need to take that tone. I came to do the decent thing. Who do you think arranged all this – old Frank over there?"

Karl looked up, surprised to see his father almost hidden behind the others.

Karl dropped his voice: "Never mind all that. I warn you I'm feeling bad. Get me a gun. I've a job to do."

"What?"

"You heard. Do it, unless you want to be on the list."

Todd recognised that ice cold obsessive stare. "All right," Todd reluctantly acceded. They shook hands.

Then Frank jumped him. "Get away from my son. You ruined one – he's dead down there – and now you've started on the other."

Todd pulled him off. " Frank, you've been drinking?"

"No, but by God I could do with one. Have you no shame man?"

Todd rolled his eyes. "Is this Frank speaking? The man with more convictions than hot dinners? It's a bit late for becoming holier than thou."

"It's never too late. So be warned. I've wasted most of my life inside and I'm not seeing it happen to Karl."

"Oh, and what are you going to do about it?"

At that Frank's old fighting spirit surfaced and he landed a punch right in Todd's middle. The two men swayed dangerously on the graveside. Then Todd doubled over, apparently all the air knocked out of him. But as Frank leant over him to strike again he head butted his opponent and sent him sprawling.

The two screws were across now and dragging them apart, while the minister, embarrassed, remonstrated with the brawlers.

"I'll get you for this," Todd spluttered when he had recovered breath. "You're not muscling back in on my patch, so don't think it."

"You, you're finished, you're a dead man," Frank called back. "I'll see you in hell for what you've done to my sons."

"Oh don't be so sanctimonious. Leave it to the minister here."

Todd pulled away from the screws. "It's all right, I'm going. I'll leave father and son to their tender reunion." Then to Karl: "Well, you remember which side your bread is buttered. That old has-been can't help you now."

Karl turned back to Frank. "Are you all right?"

Frank wiped his forehead where Todd's skull had left a bloody line. "Yes. Just a bit woozy. He's got the strength of a bull in his head." And he managed a laugh.

"Come over here," said Karl, and waving away the screw, he led Frank to a tall tombstone. "Lean on that." Then: "You should never have mixed it with Todd."

"Why not? He deserved it, the creep. I never wanted him to have anything to do with either of you. He's a parasite."

"I know Dad, but he's right, he's the only one can help me from the outside. Without him I'd have gone mad in stir."

"What do you mean? A son of mine not taking his porridge? Give over, if I could do years of it, you can."

"No Dad, I can't, and I won't."

Frank paused, and reconsidered. "Maybe you're right. I keep forgetting – you're not like me, thank God. You want a decent life and I want that for you too. More than anything."

"It's a bit late, but thanks."

"I know what you must think of me. Gary's death is partly down to me. I wasn't around to keep him out of Todd's clutches."

"Neither was I."

"That's why it is so important you don't go the same way as Gary."

Karl smiled wolfishly. "Don't worry, I won't. I can look after myself. I'm tougher than Gary. He was too nice and trusting and look where it got him."

f

"That's me. You have to be a hard bastard to survive in this world. I don't want you thinking I've gone soft because of my change of heart. That head butt of Todd's was just a lucky fluke. I'm still the man I was."

Karl didn't contradict him, though the physical deterioration was unmistakable.

The screws came over for Karl. "Come on you. Say your goodbyes."

"Take care," Frank told him. Then to Karl's utter surprise: "Gloria is waiting for me over there, with her car. She insisted."

"Dad?"

"Didn't I tell you, we're old . . . friends."

"Yes, but for goodness sake!"

The screws tapped Karl on the shoulder. "All right, all right, I'm coming. I have to go."

"Can I come to see you?"

After a pause, Karl gave a reluctant: "I suppose so."

Frank's eyes lit up. "Thanks son, you won't regret it."

"I hope not." Then Karl walked away between the two screws.

Frank, rejoicing, walked over to Gloria. "I think I'm getting through to him at last."

"I wish I could." Gloria stood wrapping her long coat around her in the breeze. Her mass of black hair flared out.

Frank admired her. Still a fine looking woman. He felt almost as if he'd bequeathed her to Karl.

"It's so frustrating," she went on. "He won't let me help him – at least not in the way I want. He's obsessed with revenge."

Frank's face hardened. "Ah, I understand that."

"Frank," Gloria began impatiently, "help me get him away from here."

"Me? How can I help?"

Gloria looked at him and wondered too. He was like a wraith, a shadow of the macho figure who used to boast of his gangland connections.

"You used to know people."

"Huh?"

"Contacts. The underworld. People who could smuggle Karl and me out of the country."

"What do I get out of this?"

"He's your son. But if you must, same as last night, only

more."

Frank's face twisted, repelled. "What do you take me for? That was for old time's sake. But two-time my own son?"

"I only meant . . . for you," Gloria tailed off. Then she rallied: "Listen Frank, I'm desperate. I have to have him. I crave him, can't you understand? Or have you forgotten all about passion along with everything else?"

Frank's spare frame tensed. "Oh I haven't forgotten a thing. Or how you dumped me whenever I was sent to prison."

"I wondered how long it would be before you dragged that one up. You couldn't expect me to wait for seven, ten years on the trot. That's madness."

"No: that's devotion. I never gave up thinking of you. But all that's in the past. If Karl wants you, that's OK. I don't begrudge him."

Gloria put her hands on her hips. "Well that's all very fine and dandy. I'm not some tart to be passed around. I have feelings."

"Look Gloria, this isn't getting us anywhere. I've changed, turned over a new leaf. I haven't any contacts any more. I've turned my back on all that."

Gloria twisted away, hurt. "I might have known. Just when I need your help you go pious on me. Well there's nothing else for it: I suppose it will have to be Todd – again."

"No Gloria, don't. Anyone but him."

Gloria turned back to Frank, eyes flashing. "Why not? You and he used to be such great buddies, years back. He's always talking of the strokes you pulled together."

"Is he? Well I prefer not to remember. We had a working partnership, but I wouldn't trust him as far as I could throw him. I've a strong suspicion he sent me over to save his own skin. One day . . ."

Gloria was scathing. "You're paranoid, jumping at shadows. What's happened to you?"

There was a pause: "I got tired, I guess. I woke up one morning and asked myself, 'what have I to show for all these years?' and all I could think of was Karl – and poor Gary, of course."

Gloria was suddenly touched. "I'm sorry Frank. You've just lost a son and I'm going on at you."

"Oh, it's all right Gloria, like old times. Remember those rows we used to have? Real up and downers. Many's the black eye you gave me."

"Did I? You never complained. You were always a real man, not like these wimps nowadays."

"I hope you don't include Karl in that?"

"Karl? No. He's like you."

Fondly she stroked Frank's rough cheek. "We could still do it, you know. Just for old time's sake."

Frank looked at her ruefully. "I never could resist a beautiful woman."

They clasped hands like young lovers and walked to Gloria's car.

Chapter Twenty-six

From the end of the street Karl had a good vantage point for observing the house where Randle had Judy holed up. At last after all the excruciating months of waiting he was about to take his revenge. Todd had reluctantly supplied him with the Browning automatic and silencer he had demanded. It hung, heavy and menacing, in his coat pocket, where harsh and cold it rested against his palm.

The alibi was the beauty of it; the police would never connect him with murder while he was serving his prison sentence, he almost giggled to himself. Then he told himself to stop becoming hysterical. But his nerves were all jangly. When he thought of Judy it was hard not to break down at the memory of her vivacious sexuality, those gleaming green eyes, that astounding figure, that electric love of life, daring any danger.

But she had betrayed him, condemned him to a seeming life-time behind bars, when one word would have saved him. She had shown him no concern or remorse for the rapid breakdown he had suffered, the awful pain and despair. What if he had committed suicide? She would have been jubilant. So he could afford no tender reminiscences.

As for Randle, a middle-aged, seedy disappointment of a man who had sold his integrity for Judy's favours – Karl had no compunction over him.

It was time. He moved off from the corner of a bus shelter and keeping low worked his way along, head down behind the privet hedges. Then he slipped along a side road, looking for a back way into Randle's house. He found the slatted wooden garden gate and carefully lifted off the latch. Then he was nimbly through and replaced it.

He skipped behind the garden shed and then worked his way up the path to the back door. He sank to his knees below the rear window and listened. The light was on, and the sound of television reached him.

Moving across he turned the handle on the back door and silently let himself in. The kitchen was dark, but he could make out the shapes of the cooker and fridge which he was careful to bypass.

Now he was pressed against the door to the living-room, the gun raised. Still the television voices rolled on. He pictured Judy and Randle relaxed together on the sofa, never suspecting that death was so close. He slowly pushed the door open and stepped inside. As his eyes adjusted to the light, Randle turned his head from the sofa and said in a tired, grating voice, "At last, we'd wondered where you'd got to. Go on: sit down over there." Then casually he switched off the television.

Karl moved quickly across the carpet to level the gun at Randle and Judy. "Don't try and make a mockery out of me. How could you be expecting me? Anyway, it doesn't matter. You'd better say your prayers."

Judy flashed her green eyes at Karl in contempt. "Do as Tom says and sit down. Put that gun away before you hurt someone."

Karl wavered. "I don't get this. You're bluffing, trying to save your skins. Well it won't work." Obstinately he stood his ground and raised the gun again. "Go on, give me one good reason why I shouldn't blast you to kingdom come."

Randle cast him a testy, and impatient look. "Because your alibi is blown."

"Why? Who could prove that I'm not in prison at this very moment?"

"I could," a soft but determined voice came from behind him.

Karl spun round. "Sarah! What are you doing here?"

"Trying to stop you making the biggest mistake of your life."

"But I don't understand. Get out of here quick, this minute."

Sarah advanced on him, her oval face open with concern, her hair pulled back. "Todd told me tonight. I couldn't let you do it. You can't kill my own sister in cold blood."

Karl waved the gun wildly, his control breaking down. "Why not? She'd let me rot for ever without lifting a finger to save me."

126

Judy sprang up. "I wouldn't. I wanted to tell . . ."

"Oh really. When? Don't you understand what you did to me?"

"Yes, it was wicked."

Sarah reached for Karl's arm. "Can't you see, we all want to help, make amends?"

Karl tore away from her. "I ought to blast everyone in this room. You're all in it together, to destroy me."

Randle stretched out his legs. "Stop making a damn fool of yourself. That gun isn't even loaded with real bullets."

"We'll see about that!" Karl pointed it at the big mirror over the fireplace and pulled the trigger. But no explosion of shattered glass followed. He tried again and again but there was only a feeble metallic click.

Furious Karl hurled the gun to one side and dived on Randle. Hands at Randle's throat he began strangling him.

"I'll finish you," Karl spluttered, pressing harder and harder.

Randle's face began purpling and his tongue was forced out. He flailed at Karl with his arms, but he was wedged against the sofa and weakening.

Then Karl felt a terrific blow on the back of his head. His skull seemed to split open and he fell back on the floor. Judy stood over him, breathing heavily, a brass candlestick in her hand.

Sarah fell down on her knees beside Karl. "You've killed him!"

"No I haven't," spat out Judy. "Have I?"

But Karl had commenced moaning and then reached behind to rub his head.

Sarah stroked his forehead and eventually helped him to sit up.

Then Karl pulled away, angry. "I can manage." He saw Judy still holding the candlestick. "Waiting to give me another wallop?"

Meanwhile Randle was massaging his neck and struggling to sit up. "You bastard," he managed. "Go on Judy, give him another one."

But Judy shook her head. Still, she gripped tight the candlestick to show she meant business. "Somebody help me up," Karl demanded.

Despite his recent rebuff, Sarah lifted him to his feet.

He rubbed his head. "I feel sick," he moaned.

"Well don't do it in here," Judy responded without sympathy.

He swayed, but then signalled them all away. "Don't touch me now. I'll be all right."

Randle stood up, his worn shirt open at the neck where marks still stood livid. "On your way, before we decide to start in on you again," he said thickly.

"Well, what happens now?" Karl asked bewildered, lost.

Sarah moved to his side. "We've a plan. Judy confided in me. Just give them time to get abroad and then we'll tell the world Judy is alive."

"So they walk away into the sunset. No deal."

Judy strutted towards him. "You're in no position to argue. One word from Sarah and your escaping days are over. They'd throw away the key."

"You'd do that to me?"

"You bet she would. You were ready to kill me a moment ago weren't you?"

"But how do I know once you're out of the country, you'd keep your end of the bargain."

Sarah intervened. "I'd make sure of it. I'm your guarantee. I'd never let you down."

"There'd have to be evidence."

"There will be – a video, letters. Whatever it takes to convince people."

"And we'll be on the run," Judy took up sourly. "It's not going to be any picnic for us."

Then Karl looked from Judy to Randle. "Well at least you'll have each other," he told them sarcastically.

"Yes, we will," Randle replied, determined. "Just don't push your luck."

"All right. I hate to see you two walking away alive but it seems I've no choice."

Sarah pulled on his arm. "Come on." She wanted him out before the fragile truce fell apart.

Judy watched him go. Then Randle turned to her. "Poor pathetic bastard with his pop-gun. Pop."

Judy turned a sour eye on Randle. "Well he damn near strangled you. Men!" Then she murmured, "Sarah only has to bat her eyelashes at Karl."

Outside Sarah guided Karl away from the house.

"I've never felt so humiliated," he complained.

"Better that than a murderer," Sarah scolded him.

"I don't know: it feels like a conspiracy."

"Listen," and Sarah stopped to make him look at her. "You don't really want to kill Judy."

"Yes I do."

"No, you want to pay her back. That's a different thing. What sort of life do you think she has with Randle?"

"Well they deserve each other."

"Exactly. She's punished herself by her choice. And what if he turns nasty on her? He's threatened to, you know."

They resumed walking. "You should have been a diplomat," Karl told her.

"Thanks, but I think all I really yearn for is a quiet life."

"What's wrong with that?"

"I don't know. Sometimes I feel I'm born to be a spectator, watching the great dramas passing me by."

Karl grinned ruefully. "Anytime you want to swop places, just say. You wouldn't want to be in my shoes. Not for anything."

"Better that than a living death."

"Hey, who's being melodramatic now? It's not like you."

"No that's the trouble. Look at me. You'd never be crazy enough about me to want to kill me."

"Count your blessings."

"No, but do you love me?"

"Of course I do. I never want to see Judy again. I hope she rots in hell."

"I'd rather you were indifferent to her."

"It's hard to be indifferent to Judy."

"See what I mean?"

Chapter Twenty-seven

With Karl safely lured away, Todd rolled slowly through the back door and joined Randle and Judy in the living-room. Hands dug deep into his overcoat pockets, he splayed his legs to occupy the floor. "There you are," he drawled. "A piece of cake. Didn't I tell you?"

Randle flared up, bitter. "It wasn't you looking down the end of that gun."

"It wasn't loaded."

"That's very comforting now. It would have been nice to be certain."

"I told you on the phone I wouldn't let him loose in here with a loaded gun. What do you take me for? I'm not crazy."

Randle scowled. "No, but he is. After firing blank he tried strangling me with his bare hands. Pity you couldn't have foreseen that!"

"Oh do stop moaning. You're alive aren't you?"

"Only thanks to me," Judy chipped in.

Todd turned to her. "Well I know I can rely on you."

"Yes, but can we rely on you?"

Todd spread his hands. "We three are standing here. I rest my case."

Randle fumed, and plumped himself down in a chair.

Exasperated Judy watched him then turned to Todd. "I think what my lover is trying to convey is: where do we go from here?"

Todd's flabby face suddenly set hard. "You don't want Karl back do you?"

"Do we hell," chimed in Randle.

"Right. Well I'm Karl's only passport out of prison. Make it worth my while and I can make sure he stays there."

"For how long?" Judy was suspicious.

"For as long as you want. For ever if that suits."

Judy debated. "I'm hard but I don't know I could do that to him."

"Well I could," Randle rounded on her.

But this only inflamed Judy: "Listen dunderhead. What we need is time – to amass some money. Living abroad doesn't come cheap. And I've no intention of grubbing about in poverty."

Todd permitted himself a smile. "Perhaps I can help you there. I've contacts: I could start you on new lives abroad."

"What's the catch?"

"Well I'd want something in return. I've a number of jobs lined up for Karl. But even with his alibi he's getting a bit hot. I'd actually prefer someone else to take over."

"Well don't look at us." Randle was riled.

"Why not?" Judy cut in. "Don't be so defeatist. With your background you ought to know how not to get caught."

"Too right, because I'm not doing it. We're in deep enough as it is. I'm not going in any further."

Todd listened impassively. "Judy?"

"Let me think about it."

"Well don't be long about it. Every day Karl is banged up useless in prison, I'm losing money."

"You'll get your money."

"I intend to. I always do."

Randle twisted round bitterly in his seat. "Go on, beat it. I've heard enough from you for one day."

Todd scowled down at him. "Don't use that tone with me. You're not a detective now. You owe me, and don't you forget it."

"Yeah, yeah."

Todd made a gesture of washing his hands of Randle. "Big man eh?" he spoke to Judy.

"Not much."

"That's what I thought. I'll see myself out," and his lumbering frame disappeared back the way he'd come.

When he had gone Judy turned to Randle. "Well you were a great help!"

But Randle was grinding his teeth. "I never would have believed it. The things you said, putting me down in front of that slug."

"Oh spare me your precious feelings. We've more important things at stake."

"Oh, I know," and he laughed bitterly. "Money, and more money. That's all I hear."

"Well it's what we need."

Randle passed a hand over his thinning hair, then withdrew it quickly and stood up. "I thought love came into it, silly old romantic that I am."

Judy scowled, uncomfortable. "Oh, come off it. We were using each other. It was convenient."

"And now?"

"Once we're out of this, we split."

"So you can't get away from me fast enough?"

"I didn't say that."

"Back to Karl, I bet. Only he's banged up. No wonder you want him out."

"Let's try and keep this civilised. No point in getting at each other's throats."

"Oh I can get a lot more worked up than this. You just watch me. I invested everything, my whole future in you, and I'm not watching it go down the tubes without a fight."

"Well you go and fight with yourself. Don't think you can frighten me. I've eaten bigger men than you for breakfast."

Randle scoffed. "Big talk, but I don't buy it."

"Tough."

Later, when Sarah had seen Karl to his vehicle, she back-tracked and returned to the house. All was quiet, Randle having taken himself off to the pub to brood and nurse his hurt pride.

Sarah let herself in the back and went upstairs to find Judy in the bedroom. "Oh, you gave me a start," and Judy jumped off the bed.

"I'm sorry Judy, only I had to come and see how things are."

"Couldn't be much worse could they?" and impulsively she reached for a hug. "I don't know what I'd do without you."

Sarah extricated herself. "Now, calmly, what's happened?"

"Todd's put the screws on us to do his dirty work."

"I loathe that man."

132

"Then to make matters worse, Tom and I fell out. I was for stringing Todd along but Randle practically threw him out with a flea in his ear. He just doesn't want to realise that we need Todd."

"So, now?"

"Tom's sulking, and I don't know what he may do. I've tried letting him down gently but he's stuck on me. I can't shake him off. It's getting to me."

"Has he threatened you?"

Judy puffed out her cheeks. "He hit me – once, and I told him not to try it again, or else. But I don't know, I don't trust him."

Sarah watched her. She knew her sister. "What are you thinking of?"

"Nothing."

"Come off it. This is bad. I can sense something."

Judy's mouth set in a hard line. "I have this awful feeling that one of us is going to wind up dead."

"Judy, don't say that. You must be crazy."

"It's just one of those middle of the night thoughts. It will probably never come to that."

Sarah looked her full in the face. "Are you sure? Look at the way you fought with Karl."

"I really stuck one on him."

"Yes, well there's no need to boast about it. Randle's different. Ex-policemen are tough."

"I can handle him."

"Start that with Randle and he's liable to finish it. Don't provoke him."

Judy sighed. "I don't like to say it, but maybe you're right. I've got to get away."

Sarah nodded.

Then Judy shook her head. But it's impossible. Out of hiding I'm finished. So I'm trapped. The only solution is to work for Todd on my own account."

"Judy! You can't. See sense."

"Sarah, I am. I've no option. He can get me away abroad, no questions asked. I know he can."

"He'll double-cross you."

"Not if I keep him sweet."

Sarah shuddered.

"Don't be so squeamish."

"I'm thinking of last time."

Judy paused. They looked at each other. Then slowly hugged. "I've no choice."

"Judy, be careful. I worry so about you."

Judy smiled and touched her cheek. "My guardian angel, eh?"

Sarah withheld a tear. "Something like that. I just wish I could make everything right for you."

"Sentimental – but nice. Like you."

"Don't. You'll set me off. Promise to speak to me before you do anything rash?"

"I promise."

Sarah nodded, but didn't believe her.

Chapter Twenty-eight

What the hell was going on? Karl seethed, waiting for Frank to arrive. Days had passed since his confrontation with Judy and Randle and nothing had changed. No summons to see the Governor, no announcement that Judy was alive and that he was a free man. No apology and recompense for the horror he'd suffered.

He should have never let Sarah soft-soap him into meekly going back. 'Trust them': that was a laugh. He'd been double-crossed. Judy and Randle would have disappeared from the house by now, destination unknown. All his proof that Judy was alive and that he was innocent had gone like a puff of smoke. Sarah had probably connived with them to save her sister from jail – or from him. Because whatever happened, however long it took, he'd get out and find those two.

He'd been oblivious to the commotion of the visitors entering the room full of tables, till Frank was standing in front of him.

"Hello son."

"Frank."

His visitor hitched up his tweed trousers and sat down. Spare framed, with a slightly concave chest, Frank still had not quite lost his own prison pallor.

"How are you?"

"Bloody mad if you must know."

"What have I done now?"

"Not you."

"Well, what then?"

Hurriedly, in a whisper, Karl outlined the events of the other evening.

"You did what?" Frank exploded.

"Keep your voice down," Karl hissed as the screws became interested.

Reluctantly Frank obliged: "Robbery's one thing. But murder. Our family's never gone in for that. No shooters, that was my motto."

Karl clicked his tongue in frustration. "Never mind a trip down memory lane. This wasn't a 'job', this was personal. But it all went wrong anyhow."

"You should never have trusted Todd. I've warned you till I'm tired about that man. I might have known he'd slip you a phoney gun."

"Yes, well all that's not much consolation now."

"No, but perhaps you've learnt your lesson."

Karl looked up towards the ceiling. "Give me strength. Will you stop going pious on me? I want help not advice."

Frank leant forward, his lined face grave and concerned. "All right, only I hate to see you repeating my mistakes."

Karl nodded. "OK. But listen, I need you to find out what's going on. Here's the address Judy and Randle were at. Check it out, would you, and see if they're still there? Even though I know they'll have skipped. And see Todd. Find out what he knows."

Frank gave a warning stare. "Todd?"

"That's right. Try not to have another punch up. Once was enough, him doubled up over the grave. With a bit of luck, I thought, he'd topple in."

Frank grinned back grimly. "Yeh, an early grave would be about right for him, after . . ." then he paused and put his hand up. "All right, I can take a hint. No trouble. I'll keep my temper – so long as he doesn't provoke me."

"Frank, don't louse this up. I don't like Todd any more than you do but I need him working for me. Don't turn him against me. Understand?"

"As if I would. What do you take me for? I'd cut off my right arm for you. You know that."

"Yes, well don't make rash promises. That won't be necessary."

"I want to make up for the past."

"I just don't know Frank."

"But me being here, us talking like this. It's a start isn't it?"

Wearily he agreed: "Yes, it's a start."

"I'll pump Todd for you. He and I go back a long way."

"I wonder about that. Todd's never struck me as the sentimental type."

"Trust me son. I'll think of something. Always was quick at thinking on my feet."

"So the judges said," Karl replied dead pan.

"Joke eh? Yes, that's good. Well I'll go now. Don't want to overstay my welcome. See you son."

"See you," then Karl had to give him the word he craved, "Dad."

Frank looked away embarrassed but warmed, pretending not to give it heed. "Aye," and he was gone, a stringy, loping figure, heading fast for the exit. Karl would never know the effort of will he had made to voluntarily enter a prison again to visit his son.

Later that day found Frank squaring his shoulders and entering Todd's 'clinic'. He brushed quickly through the inner door which led to Todd's consulting room.

Todd looked up from some papers with a suspicious and belligerent stare. "What do you want? Make an appointment if you want to see me."

Frank pulled out a chair and sat down. "Cut the crap Harold. We know each other too well for all that."

"So?" Todd leaned back till his beer belly swelled over his belt.

"I've come because Karl asked me."

"Sent you."

"Asked me. Don't rile me Harold. Where are Judy and Randle?"

Todd spread his hands.

Frank glared at him, frustrated. "I've tried their last address and there's no sign of them. Neighbours said the house was empty."

"So how should I know?"

"Because you put them up to it. It's got all your hallmarks. Karl told me about the other night and the neutered gun."

Todd smiled and wiped his palms together. "I couldn't let the lad loose killing people, now could I? He just had to get it out of his system. He won't try anything as silly again."

"Don't you count on it. The longer you let him rot in prison the more steamed up he'll get."

137

"Me? What have I to do with it? I didn't put him away."

"No, but you can spring him fast enough when it suits."

Todd's podgy face twisted in anger. "I did the lad a favour, which is more than you've ever done. So don't come it. He was grateful just to be out, for a night. You should have seen his face."

"Well now he wants justice. He's seen Judy alive."

"He'll have it. But he'll just have to be patient. There isn't just him to consider."

"He's my son and that's all I'm interested in."

"You should have thought of that sooner, shouldn't you? I kept your cover remember, when people thought you were dead."

Frank looked uncomfortable. "Yes, well, thanks. We had a deal."

"And I kept my part. So where's the money?"

"What money?"

"Don't play the innocent. The treasure trove from all those jobs. The money that never got shared out. You buried it. And I want it. It's my due."

"There is no buried fortune. This is just crazy. It's all in your imagination."

Todd seethed; his long, flat cauliflower ears reddening. "Don't you dare patronise me. I know there's buried loot. It's no secret."

"It is to me."

"You mean you won't tell me."

"I mean there's nothing to tell."

Todd rose and rested his fat stumpy arms on the desk. "Don't give me that. I warn you Frank, I've waited a long time for this. I've covered for you, I've looked after that boy of yours like a father. Now it's time to pay the bill."

Frank had risen too, and stood lively like a boxer on his toes, ready for anything. "Harold, watch my lips. I have no fortune stashed away anywhere. If I had you'd be welcome to it. I've put that kind of life behind me."

"So just tell me where it is, and I'll take it off your hands."

"Harold, you've not been listening. There's nothing there."

Todd began to pace, his brow furrowed. "All those months when you were playing dead and I was covering for you, what were you doing?"

"What is all this Harold? I don't see the point."

"Bear with me. Well?"

"Doing? Laying low most of the time. Getting my head together."

"Seeing old lady friends? Making up for lost time while banged up in the nick. Getting your leg over?"

Frank's face became stony with disgust. "Yes, some of the time. I didn't live like a monk. But quite what dragging up my sex life has to do with anything?"

"Well it just strikes me that you and Karl follow the same pattern. You both go for the same women. Gloria for instance."

"Gloria and I are just old friends."

"Oh yes? And all the others. All those poor dead middle-aged ladies. Now if Karl didn't kill them, who else knew them all?"

Frank's eyes popped in amazement. He was dumfounded and then: "You're mad!"

"Why couldn't it be you? You've been banged up most of your life. Chronically frustrated. Angry. Seeing your son Karl getting all the women you'd lusted over in your cell and couldn't have. So you killed them."

"I never. Take that back."

"Where's your alibis?"

"Alibis? For all that time ago?"

"Exactly. You have none. You were laying low. Your movements a secret."

Light dawned on Frank. "Oh, I see. You're setting me up."

"I don't have to. You're made for it. I'm amazed the police never put you in the frame. Still Karl was a stronger bet. And they may have believed the newspapers that you were dead."

"But you'd soon tell them I'd been resurrected."

Todd moved towards him. "Frank, I've never put the finger on anyone in my life. I'm not a stool pigeon. You don't live long if you are, I've learned that. No, I've just a proposition for you. That's all."

"Hang on a minute. Suppose I was the killer. Wouldn't it bother you?"

"I've told you before Frank, I don't moralise like you. I'd do business with the devil if it paid."

"So what's this proposition?"

"You tell me where the money is and I'll guarantee you and Karl a life of luxury away from prisons. What do you say?"

"What if there is no money?"

"Frank, cut the pretence. Let's not go through all that again."

"If that's your offer I'd better go. Shall I pass on your good regards to Karl?"

"You do what you like. But you think about it and don't take too long. I want a result – one way or another."

"I can still take you Harold. Don't you forget it. I ran that gang, not you. I gave the orders. I can do it again, if I have to."

"Which way are you wearing your collar today? Hadn't you better make up your mind?"

Frank smiled, showing his teeth. "I like to keep you guessing. See you Harold."

"Oh yes, you'll see me, Frank. I'll never be far away. Remember that."

Chapter Twenty-nine

Judy, in black ribbed top and skirt, confronted Todd in his office: "Well, am I in?"

Todd sat back in his chair perplexed. "What?" I wish you'd stop bursting in here and disturbing me when I'm trying to work."

Judy swayed her hips provocatively. "Stop stalling. You remember our conversation all right."

Then a light seemed to go out in her eyes to be replaced by a terrible sadness. "Harold, I'm in a hole and you've got to help me. I need money so badly."

"Well I'm not giving it to you if that's what you're thinking."

Judy was stung. "Have I ever sought something for nothing in my life? Never. So you can wipe that smug expression off your face."

Todd was becoming weary: "All right Judy what is it you want?"

"One of those jobs you talked about. A chance to make a lot of money fast."

"You and your ex-policeman? You must be kidding."

"You didn't seem to think so the other day."

"That was then. I've had time to think. There are at least two counts against you: I can't trust him and I can't rely on you."

Judy forced herself not to get angry, but still she bristled, her green eyes narrowing. "You can drop Randle from the picture. This is strictly me, solo."

"Even so, look how you bungled it last time, using your own car on a hold-up. How stupid can you get?"

"Are you trying to rile me or what? Because you're doing a very good job. That was just me showing off to Karl, that time. I

141

can be professional, as good as any man. Better."

"And you want a chance to prove it?"

Judy leaned towards him over the desk. "Precisely. I can be very grateful, as you know."

"Yes, well that's all very tempting. But maybe I'd better stick to Karl. He's pulled off all the jobs so far. And he has the alibi."

"But you said yourself it's becoming too hot for him. His luck can't hold for ever. I'm sure you could work out an alibi for me."

Todd thought. "That might be arranged. But I'd want my usual cut of the takings."

"How much?"

"Fifty per cent."

"What! How am I supposed to hide away abroad on what's left?"

"Take it or leave it."

"I'll case my own job."

"Be my guest."

She leant forward and fondled his lapel. "Oh, come on Harold. You can see how I'm fixed."

"No."

Then her long arms were round his neck and she was shaking him. "Harold. I'm desperate. I've got to get away from Randle before he kills me. He's as jealous as hell."

Todd disentangled himself roughly. "Then what are you doing here? If he's followed you . . ."

"He doesn't know about us."

"He'd better not. Ex-policemen often keep their contacts. He might turn us both over."

"He can't. Not after conspiring to put Karl behind bars."

Todd stroked his double chin. "Maybe. But I don't trust him. He's always had it in for me. Perhaps it's time to frighten him off so he leaves you and me alone for good."

Judy's eyes glistened with hope. "Would you? I'd be so grateful. He gives me the creeps. He sticks to me like a limpet."

"Then we must prize him off, mustn't we?"

"Sounds good." Then her eyes narrowed again. "But if you've any ideas of taking his place, forget it. I've had my bellyful of men."

"Perhaps you've never had one who treated you properly."

"And you're the man to do it, I suppose?"

"I could give you a life beyond your wildest dreams."

"Now where have I heard that before? Oh yes, from Tom Randle. You'll have to do better than that."

"But you don't understand. I can deliver. He never could. He's just a broken down old copper headed for the knackers' yard."

"And you're a struck-off middle-aged GP. Where's the difference?"

Todd placed a fat hand upon her forearm and his breath was heavy over her. "Anything, anybody I want I get."

Judy wrenched her arm away. "Don't threaten me."

"Stop being so uppity. You're in no position."

Judy gathered up her belongings. "I'm leaving. I'm not stopping to listen to this. I don't know why I came. I'd be better off with Randle."

"Fine. There's the door. You go back to him."

Then Judy turned on Todd: "No. I'll manage on my own, and damn you all. See if I don't!" And she stalked defiantly out of the door.

Chapter Thirty

Weeks, and nothing. Weeks of staring at the cell walls, of doing his 'recreation', of slopping out, of Robinson shaking his head, of thinking: when? When would the word come? "Judy is known to be alive. You are free and pardoned. A thousand apologies."

Instead nothing; no word, not even Judy and Randle's whereabouts from Frank. They had disappeared off the face of the earth and he was left to look like an idiot. He'd had his chance to be revenged, to get even, to be free and he'd blown it. He'd allowed himself to be tricked, to be led through the nose by Todd and Sarah unprotesting back into prison.

But this time they meant him to stay there. He'd served his purpose, done Todd's jobs for him and kept him in the clear. However, since he'd turned vengeful, they'd banged him up and thrown away the key.

It was a terrible feeling, that the rest of them were getting on with their lives, while he was out of it, discarded, a nobody. That hurt the most.

Years in prison had done it to his father, knocked the stuffing out of Frank. Well it wasn't happening to him. He was getting out of there, for good, before he became a vegetable, a mental case, with no will of his own.

Being alone in his hilltop cave retreat was one thing, but solitary in his oppressive cell was quite another. No matter how loud he cried out no one in the outside world could hear him.

He needed to be able to make a commotion, cause a stir, just to prove he was alive. Those jobs he'd done for Todd had briefly given him that feeling of exhilaration. But that was all over, he was redundant now and there was total silence from Todd.

It was all down to himself, now. All the rest – Sarah, Frank, Todd – had failed him. Gary was dead. He had only his own reserves to draw on. But they'd always underestimated him. The lot of them. They thought he was a lightweight, a prankster, a country Casanova with older women. Well he'd show them.

He had to get out – but without Robinson, the screw, smoothing his path. The bastard had turned him down, on orders from Todd: "Not yet." Not ever, more like.

No: he needed an entirely fresh escape plan, and this place was like a fortress. Nor could he rely on any help from outside. He couldn't break out – so the only alternative was to get the authorities to do it for him. Gary's funeral would have been a perfect opportunity, but it was too late now.

But maybe Gary in death could still help him in a way he never could alive. It was a bitter thought but Karl knew that Gary would have wanted to help. He was like that; selfless. Karl worried endlessly over the details for days and then took the plunge. He went to see the Governor.

It meant implicating Gary in the attack on the Chief Constable's house, but that couldn't hurt Gary now, he told himself. The issue was so hot that Karl's testimony was immediately top priority. Karl's alibi kept him in the clear but his information gained 'from his visitors' about Gary's role was considered invaluable as a lead.

Karl's request to assist enquiries was accepted. He was to be escorted to Gary's lodgings on the pretext of him pointing out a secret cache of tear gas grenades and fire-arms.

The day dawned grey when Karl was hustled into a police car. He was wearing civvies at his insistence and that of the Chief Constable who was sitting beside him. The man was bald, dignified, with heavy jowls and a sour expression.

"I'm not having you showing me up. Now behave yourself and for your sake this better not be any wild goose chase. Are you sure you didn't have anything to do with this?"

"On my honour, how could I? I'm not some criminal mastermind orchestrating things from inside. I'm an ordinary bloke whose wife did a disappearing act to pin a murder on me."

The Chief Constable yawned. "Yes all right, your alibi tallies but please spare me the innocence routine. I've heard it too many times."

g

Karl managed a hurt look. "Just because every con says it doesn't mean it's not true of me."

"At the moment I want to know who attacked my home and officers. Find me your brother's accomplice and I might listen."

"It's all right for you."

"That's enough. Driver, hurry it will you? We haven't got all day."

The car eventually pulled up outside a low rise block of flats. Water damage was visible on some of the panels and the gardens were a dumping ground. As they climbed out, a second car arrived and more police officers congregated.

"Now," the Chief Constable began severely to Karl, "we've been over this flat since you told us, and found nothing."

Karl eyes him deadpan. "I'm not surprised. You don't know where to look."

An officer tapped him on the shoulder. "All right, clever clogs. Suppose you show us. Surprise us all."

Karl led the way, thinking feverishly. He made a show of going over Gary's flat, all the while followed by suspicious and impatient eyes.

"Well?" the officer said. "Don't be bashful."

"No need for sarcasm. I'm doing my best."

"And I've got the Chief Constable outside. He'll blow a gasket and I'll catch it if there's nothing to show."

"All right, keep your hair on. Have you tried these waste disposal panels at the back of the kitchen?"

The officer came forward and then motioned to his colleagues. While they delved, Karl withdrew and indicated the wall. "Gary used to stash stuff down the waste disposal. He'd fixed it so it wouldn't work. The tubing runs down behind this wall."

The kitchen was soon a flurry of activity with even the Chief Constable nosing about and getting in everybody's way.

Karl seized his chance, tucked himself away for a moment behind the kitchen door, and then slipped down the 'garbage corridor' as it was known, where all the dust bins and cleaning equipment were kept.

Helter skelter he flew down the enclosed space, tripping over bottles and plastic containers on the way, till he was scrambling out at the bottom. He emerged behind low brick outhouses, and body bent, worked his way along to the fence by the side. Then vaulting over it, he was running for dear life down the entry and into the side road.

He threaded his way across town trying to hurry without actually running and drawing attention to himself. He knew he had only minutes as the alarm call for his recapture would have been sent out.

Fortunately his appearance was nondescript in his civvies and he looked no different from hundreds of other men busily keeping appointments in the town. He was determined to keep his nerve and not flinch or become awkward at the sight of a uniform. This discipline kept him moving purposefully towards his goal: Sarah's greenhouses. This time of day was her busiest and he was counting on finding her there.

The dual carriageway came into view, and he had only to cross it to reach the greenhouses and allotments on the other side. But he had to climb the pedestrian bridge first. Up there he would be visible, exposed, and trapped.

Looking from side to side he thought he was safe. Gulping he gripped the chilly metal rail and clambered up. His feet rang out a tattoo as he hastened up and on to the top. Once there he seemed to be paralysed. His luck couldn't hold, something was bound to go wrong. He looked down at the road, and felt dizzy. He leant on the rail and he thought he was going to be sick.

"Hey, what are you doing?" a voice came up from way below on the pavement.

Horror-struck, Karl scanned below looking for its source. He had been spotted.

Then he found the man: burly, young, wearing a gaberdine coat. "Nothing, I'm OK," Karl responded.

The man looked doubtful. "Yes, well don't do anything daft will you?"

And he waited and watched as Karl hurried along the top and down on the other side. Eventually, satisfied he moved off.

As Karl made for cover he cursed his weakness up there, and prayed the police wouldn't trace the witness. Putting the fence between him and the carriageway he leant his back against it and breathed heavily. All these months of heart-stopping forays out of prison had taken their toll. Yet this was the big one: for good this time. So he had to hold together.

Edging his way along, he forced himself to walk naturally

147

again as he could be seen from the allotments. Then the greenhouses came into view and he strained his eyes.

Then, peace. She was there, red bandana in her hair, working away with her graceful methodical movements.

He clambered down the bank and then circled behind the allotment huts before coming out at the first greenhouse. Through the glass he could see Sarah close up. She appeared as if in one of those misted photographs, head lowered intently, peasant blouse a field of turquoise and green, her skirt draped over curved tanned legs, feet in moccasins.

"Sarah," he mouthed. Just to produce the name, for pleasure. Then he came round and entered her greenhouse.

"Sarah."

She spun round, her hand clutched to her throat. "Please don't do that. I'm a nervous wreck, with people creeping up on me."

"I'm sorry. But I don't have much time."

"You've escaped again."

"But this time it's for good. With no help from Todd."

Sarah was shocked. "So you're really on the run? And you come to me. Are you mad? The police will be here at any minute."

Karl's eyes bore down on her. "Give me some credit. I know they'll check you out. I can only stay a moment."

Sarah's face opened in appeal: "What do you want of me? What can I do?"

"Let me sleep rough around here. Bring me food when I need it."

"Sleep in the greenhouses?"

"Why not?"

Sarah thought aloud. "I suppose I could leave the heat on. We could fix up a sort of crib for you underneath the benches with the seed trays."

"And with those boxes and bags of fertiliser to hide me, the police wouldn't spot me, even with flashlights."

"You'd be terribly uncomfortable."

"That's the least of my worries. I just need somewhere to kip down at night. During the day I'll be on the move."

Sarah came close and gazed up at him, her normally serene brow lined. "What are you up to Karl?"

148

"Meaning?"

"Why aren't you clearing straight out of the area? You're looking for Judy."

"What if I am? She's disappeared. Do you know where she is?"

"No, and if I did I wouldn't tell you. You're going to try and kill her again."

"Nonsense." But his denial was half-hearted.

"Karl, you must get this revenge nonsense out of your head. Killing Judy wouldn't do any good. And the whole idea is horribly wrong. In fact, I don't even know why I'm talking to you."

"Because you love me."

Sarah sniffed back a tear. "Maybe. But I'd do anything to stop you killing my sister."

"Including shopping me to the police?"

Sarah was near breaking down. "Please Karl, I can't bear it. You're tearing me in two. Don't make me choose between you. Thankfully she's gone and you'll never find her."

"So you'll hide me?"

After a pause: "Yes. But promise me you'll not hurt Judy. If only you'd waited you would have been proved innocent and released."

Karl scowled in disbelief. "When? With Judy disappeared? Never."

"Still: promise me."

"I promise," he lied.

"Now hold me, then go Karl. I don't think I can stand much more of this. I'm not cut out for it."

"You're doing fine," Karl murmured as he kissed her.

"Am I? Am I coming up to scratch? I don't know, I don't believe I am. That's always been my trouble."

"You've not let me down so far."

"No I haven't, have I?" Then she balked tearfully: "But why have you dragged me into all this? You're making me unhappy, do you understand? I never thought a man would do that to me again."

"Life's hard. Painful."

"Yes, but it doesn't have to be."

"All right," and Karl soothed her, stroking her hair. "I'll try and

149

keep it away from you, all the bad stuff. Will that satisfy you?"

"I just want us to be together, with all this pain behind us."

"It will be, one day."

"Will it? I tell myself that, but I'm not sure I really believe it."

Chapter Thirty-one

That night Karl lay shivering in a sleeping-bag amidst the seed trays, gnawing a chicken leg like a starving dog. Savagely he tore off strips of flesh to assuage his hunger and anger. As a fugitive he'd spent the day keeping one step ahead of the police whilst trawling the cafés and pubs for information of Judy and Randle. His nerves were rubbed raw and yet he had come up with nothing. They seemed to have dropped off the edge of the planet. No one had heard anything, or they weren't telling him. Maybe Todd had put the fix in.

It was no use badgering Sarah. He was convinced she knew nothing, and despite her better judgement she was hiding him. He shouldn't have involved her but what option did he have? Besides, Judy was bound to contact her sooner or later, and then he'd have his revenge.

Dropping the eaten chicken leg he fondled the razor-sharp pruning knife he'd found. The blade stung against his thumb. When he found Judy he was going to stick it in her and twist it, the bitch, for all she'd put him through.

But he couldn't if she was nowhere to be found. "Judy, where the hell are you?" he cursed into space.

His thoughts went back to Sarah: she was his one reliable source of information. Surely Judy would have been in touch by now? After all she had disappeared days ago. Besides, those two were supposed to be almost telepathic. Suppose Sarah did know something and was hiding it from him to protect Judy. But he'd know, he could tell, Sarah was transparent – wasn't she?

He began to doubt his own judgement and knowledge of people. After all, he would never have dreamed that Judy could do all this to him.

The suspense was agony. Sarah had dropped off the food hours ago and he wouldn't see her again until tomorrow evening. He couldn't wait that long. If he didn't get some news of Judy to act on he'd go demented. He felt like a stray animal, slinking about the town streets, rejected. To have sunk so low after his glittering life as a London photographer, rubbing shoulders with the famous. Now he was scavaging like a hunted animal.

His mind was made up: whatever the risk, he was going up to the flat. He had to see Sarah, confront her, talk to someone before he cracked up.

Wriggling out of his sleeping-bag, quickly he was fully dressed again and then warily sneaking away from the greenhouses. It would be just his luck to be picked up by the police on the street, but in fact his walk to the flats was unchallenged.

He paused on the corner opposite: everything looked normal with just two windows in the block illuminated. Padding across the road, he quickly entered the lobby and headed up the stairs. His head popped round the final flight – to see a cluster of police officers emerging from Sarah's flat.

Shocked he withdrew and almost fell over himself trying to retreat unnoticed. Terrified he looked behind him, but no one was following. They'd be upon him any minute. He hoisted himself down by the banister rail till he came to the stairwell.

Desperate he slunk back into the farthermost shadowed corner and crouched down, making himself as small as possible. His breathing sounded terribly loud to him in the suffocating silence down there.

But all was soon disturbed by the hammering sound of boots on stairs as the police squad descended towards him. He crouched in terror as they converged in his direction, and then pounded through and out in the night.

Breathless he waited and listened for any return: terrible minutes of doubt and trepidation that he might still be discovered. When would it ever be safe to emerge? He couldn't stay there all night.

The minutes lengthened and still nothing happened. Could it be a trap? He scolded himself not to be silly, and after several minutes more forced himself to emerge from his hiding place and take a look.

He peered into the lobby and then through the open door to the street. It seemed empty.

He was about to run for it, and then changed his mind. What if Sarah had broken down and directed the police to the greenhouses? Anywhere on the streets would be dangerous for him now, if they knew he was in the vicinity. In that case the flat was his only refuge.

Besides, he had to find out what Sarah had told the police, even if he had to shake it out of her. He was getting used to betrayal, he told himself grimly, as he ascended again.

He rapped firmly on the door. Sarah called out, "Not again please. I can't take any more." But she reluctantly opened up.

Then, eyes wide: "Karl! for God's sake."

"I know. I've just seen the police leave." He barged in.

Angrily Sarah slammed the door behind him. "You must be mad, coming here."

"Never mind all that," Karl snapped, hard faced. "What have you told the police?"

Sarah's face fell, confused.

"Come on, out with it. You shopped me, didn't you? It's written all over you. Women."

Sarah's face came up blazing. "You've a high opinion of me haven't you? I didn't tell them anything."

"Oh no?"

"No, they came to tell me something. Judy's been arrested."

"What?" Karl was completely thrown.

"Apparently she was copying you, doing a robbery which went wrong."

Karl slumped down in an armchair. "I can't believe it. Are you making this up?"

"Of course not. I wouldn't invent something like that about my own sister. The police were asking me if I knew anything about it, which I didn't."

"Todd will have put her up to it, after side-lining me. Serves them both right. Incompetence."

"Well this lets you off the hook, and puts my sister in prison."

Karl stared at her: "Well? You don't expect me to be sorry for her, do you?"

Sarah pushed her hair back. "No, I suppose not. But stop looking so smug. It's all horrible. Still you'll have your freedom now."

153

"You bet. But I won't have one thing."

"What's that?"

"My revenge. That bitch has put herself out of my reach. I might have known it. I should have done for her when I had the chance."

Sarah shuddered. "Don't talk like that. You can't mean it. Don't you want to be pardoned, free?"

She gulped, almost about to cry. "Why can't you think of me for a change? Have you any idea what it does to me to hear you talking like that. Sometimes I think you've no feelings for me at all."

"Sarah, that's not true."

"Then why all this pent up feeling about Judy? If you hate her so, you must love her too."

"That's crazy talk. I just want to pay her back then never set eyes on her again."

"Supposing you'd killed her?"

"Then good riddance."

"Don't Karl, that's chilling. I think you'd better go now. I don't think I recognise you. Maybe I've been wrong about you all along. You're obsessed. You don't love me. You don't love anyone."

"Sarah, please."

But she turned away and fled into the bedroom. "Just go," she called out. "I can't bear you around me. Don't touch me again."

Angry, frustrated, Karl glared at her, all his elation destroyed. "All right. But I'll be back. You've not seen the last of me."

Chapter Thirty-two

As Karl walked out into the night, dark mists of death seemed to hover around him. Suddenly it all came flooding back: his lovers murdered, Gary dead, and a lethal weapon in his hand. He seemed fated to join that grim procession.

All his dead lovers: what part had he played in their killing? He still didn't know what he might have done in those drug-crazed rites. Maybe he had blotted it all out since. It couldn't be coincidence that all his lovers ended up murdered. He must be implicated somehow.

Then there was poor dependent Gary, so easily led and impressed. If it weren't for him, Gary wouldn't have fallen under Todd's spell and died.

Karl felt the guilt of the survivor. With Judy in custody his own pardon must be assured, yet what would he do with his freedom when he got it? He felt no elation now but only fury that Judy's arrest had put her beyond his reach. He wanted to tear her heart out.

Despite her being in custody, there must be a way to get to Judy. Who would know how? As always there was one person for a dirty job: Todd.

Never mind that Todd had betrayed him, left him to die in prison when once he had served his purpose. Time was short and only Todd could deliver.

Anxiously Karl hailed a taxi and headed for Todd's home. So what that it was the middle of the night. It would serve the old devil right to be woken up.

At his destination Karl jumped out, paid off the cabby, and ran to the door. It was an ordinary red brick semi, well guarded from prying eyes by privet hedges and doing nothing to draw attention to itself or its owner.

Karl kept his finger on the bell till a disgruntled and bleary-eyed Todd answered the door. He was swathed in a crimson dressing gown.

"What the hell? Oh it's you. Do you know what time it is?"

"Never mind that. Do you want the rest of the street to hear?"

Reluctantly Todd made way for Karl to barge in. Then shutting the door firmly he said, "We'd better talk in the lounge."

It was incongruously furnished with a peach, veloured three piece suite, French heavily ornamented drinks cabinet, and a black state of the art TV. This was not the room of a family man.

"Well?" Todd had planted himself on the sheepskin hearth-rug and was warming himself after lighting the gas fire. "You'd better have a damn good reason for dragging me out of bed at this unearthly hour."

"I've been kept awake lots of nights at this hour, in my cell."

"Oh lord preserve us. Not that again."

"Just so you don't forget. It's easy to, when you're out here wheeling and dealing. I heard not a dicky-bird from you after that last job."

Todd stirred uneasily. "It wasn't the right time. You were getting too hot."

"With my alibi? No, your screw Robinson told me how you'd put the block on."

"It was for your own good."

"Come off it, when did you ever do anything which didn't serve Harold Todd?"

"And I suppose you're a shining example of unselfishness? Get to the point. I'm tired."

"Since you don't want to socialise I will. Judy's been arrested."

Todd sighed. "I know, stupid girl. She wanted to do a job for me. I turned her down, but she went ahead anyway. She was picked up with the stuff on her. Amateurs!"

"You didn't by any chance tip off the police?"

"No I did not. What a suggestion. I'm not an informer."

"All right, skip it. I'm not that bothered. Do you know where they are holding her?"

Todd's piggy eyes narrowed. "What do you care? Now the police have her, alive and well, your pardon is only a matter of time."

Karl stiffened, tense. "Yes, but I can't wait. If I turn myself in, I have to go back to prison and pay for my escape. I won't be walking free, awhile."

"So, it might take a few weeks, months at most."

Karl jumped up and grabbed Todd by his dressing-gown collar. "Don't you understand, I can't wait that long. I have an appointment with Judy, a date that must be kept. Time is running out."

Todd dragged Karl's hands away. "Don't be so emotional. What is all this? You can't see her, now she's in police custody and that's an end to it. So you might as well get all thoughts of revenge out of your head."

Exasperated, Karl prowled the room. Turning he said, "Will you let me worry about that? Just find out where she is."

Casually Todd looked down, contemptuously. "Oh I know that already."

"So? Tell me."

"Why should I? You're likely to do something rash. Besides what's in it for me?"

"Todd, believe me, I'm not leaving until you tell me. You owe me – all those jobs I pulled for you. Then dropping me like a stone."

Todd considered. Besides, he didn't like the desperation in Karl's eyes. "Perhaps you're right. Anyway, the information's not worth much to me. She's being held on remand in that open prison just outside town. Lucky for her she hadn't gone armed. Then she really would have been banged up.

"Thanks." Karl couldn't restrain his gratitude. Why was it that awful people were often the most use?

"I'm glad you're pleased. Now will you go, and let me get some sleep? I've a busy day tomorrow."

Heading for the front door, Karl turned and grinned. "So have I."

Then he was gone, out into the night.

Chapter Thirty-three

Todd stumbled upstairs to bed but he couldn't sleep. They were all coming back to haunt him: first Frank, now Karl. The son was running around like a loose cannon. When he discovered the authorities wouldn't let him see Judy he was likely to go berserk. He might say or do anything, and implicate Todd in the process.

Frank would now do anything for his son, including sending Todd over if it would help. Or maybe Frank had ambitions to run the gang again and rescue his old share of the profits.

What about the buried loot that everyone denied? He knew it existed: Frank was the canny kind; he would have salted away his money. But where? It drove Todd mad to think that probably nearby in the locality, under his very nose, existed a king's ransom. Enough to set him up for life, to retire and live in grandeur.

There was one question, though, that troubled him: why hadn't Frank unearthed the fortune himself and disappeared with it? But of course: his longed-for son prevented it. Probably he was biding his time. After all, he had waited all these years.

Todd rubbed his stubby fingers together as he sat up in bed. He'd tried everything with Frank and Karl: bluff, cajolery, threats, promises, but all to no avail. Not getting what he wanted was a new, unpleasant experience. Worse, it opened a terrifying prospect that he was not all-powerful in this town, that there were people who could defy him and get away with it.

His fleshy lips pursed: if that ever got around, others might follow their example. He had something on most people who mattered, but still not everyone. Let his stranglehold slip for an instant and they'd begin to wriggle free, and maybe talk.

No, he had to re-assert his authority, and beat off any challenge from Frank before it could gain momentum.

Dawn was breaking, and he was now clear-eyed and determined. He showered and dressed in one of his smartest double-breasted suits with a white shirt, fake old school tie, and silver tie pin.

After breakfast he waited at the table, fingers interlaced, brooding until he was able to phone Frank and arrange a meeting. Reluctantly Frank agreed.

Late that morning Todd sidled into the back room of the Queen's Head, a mottled-brick pub with long rectangular windows, a leaking flat roof, and plywood on the walls. It was a characterless box functional only for drinking and playing fruit machines.

The room was empty and Todd had made it known to the landlord that he wanted it to stay that way. There were dull green upholstered benches round the walls and small dark wood tables and stools dotted about. Todd had braced himself on the bench against one of the walls facing the door. His hands rested on his knees. He could wait.

Presently Frank's spare, bony white face showed round the door and he entered light on his feet, but not so agile any more. He sat on a stool opposite Todd. "Well, are you buying?"

"What's your pleasure?"

"Pint."

Todd rose slowly, working his way round to the bar and soon returned with the pints. He sat down again and they both drank deep and silently.

Then Todd resumed, "It takes you back – here."

"Does it?"

"What, have you forgotten? The Overton job. Our best. It was all planned on that table over there."

"All right keep your voice down. You're taking a chance, talking like this? What's come over you?"

Todd folded his arms impassively. "Oh it's safe as houses in here. Say anything. The landlord's in my pocket."

"Oh, like everyone else."

"Almost everyone."

Frank raised an eyebrow and drank again from his pint. "I was never in your pocket."

"I know, we were partners."

"So – what are you suggesting? That we resume where we left off?"

"What do you think of the idea?"

"Me? As they say, this is all so sudden."

"Well?"

"I suppose it has its attractions."

"Are you in?"

"I could be."

"And what about those new scruples?"

"Maybe I could be persuaded to forget them."

"Are you playing me along?"

"What do you think?" Frank said evenly.

"I think you could be a dirty police informer here to grass on me."

Frank's face went even whiter than before. "Take that back."

"Why?"

"Because it's not true and you know it. I've never done that."

"No." Todd paused to think. "No, maybe you're right."

"Damn well believe it."

Todd put up his hands. "OK no need to get so aerated. I was just testing you out."

Frank smoothed down his collar and drank again. "No need for that."

"But there is, if we're to resume our partnership."

"You keep talking about that, not me."

"Don't you want to?"

"I'd never thought about it."

"Well think about it now."

"What if I said yes?"

Todd's voice sank to a threatening bass. "I'd call you a liar."

"What?"

Todd half rose and leant across to Frank: "You're not coming back, ever. I know your little game. Partners? Never: you'd have to be top dog again."

"You've got it all wrong," Frank snarled back, scraping his chair. "You're the one who has to be top dog. But you're right. I have been playing you along. I'm not going to join with you – I'm going to wipe you off the face of the earth."

Todd was so surprised that he involuntarily sat back.

"You think that after what you've done to Gary and Karl I'd have anything to do with you? Scum, that's what you are and you're finished in this town. I'll see to that."

"So you are a police rat."

Frank stretched out his forefinger. "No I'm not. But there are other ways. I've not forgotten all my old tricks. I'll put you away, personally."

"You're over-reaching yourself," Todd replied with deadly calm, and holding Frank's wrist with one hand, with the other took a pub steak knife and stabbed Frank through the heart.

Shock and horror convulsed Frank's features. He scrabbled with his hand at the knife but it was embedded too deeply.

Then Todd released his other hand, and Frank fell back against the chair and on to the floor, twitching like a stuck pig. Then he stopped, eyes staring.

Thinking quickly Todd buttoned up Frank's jacket over the knife hilt to hide it. Then he lifted the body, and placed one arm over his shoulder as if he were removing a drunk. He staggered out of the back door, dragged Frank's body across the car park, and pushed it into his car.

He drove carefully across town till he reached the deserted, broken down shell of the petrol station from where he had so often sent Karl off on jobs.

He dumped the body in the remains of the cashier's office. Then sweating furiously from all this exertion freed himself to drive to the nearest phone box.

There he made two calls: one to Sarah with an urgent message for Karl, and the other to the police. As he emerged dabbing his forehead he congratulated himself on a nice clean operation. No need to even change his suit.

"That'll cook Karl's goose," he smiled to himself, and then suddenly mention of food made him feel hungry. He'd built up a real appetite.

Chapter Thirty-four

After confronting Todd, Karl had returned to Sarah's flat and prevailed upon her, half asleep as she was, to share her bed. Too tired to argue she had conceded that if he was prepared to risk discovery then she was.

In the morning he was evasive about his next move, but Sarah knew: he was fixated on finding a way to get to Judy.

"Why can't I be enough for you? Didn't our lovemaking mean anything?"

But Karl just shrugged and didn't answer. She longed to shake him, to beat him about the shoulders with her fists, to make him turn and pay attention to her. Instead she sulked and hung around the kitchen, ghost-like.

Then came Todd's phone call and with a tired, uninterested voice she passed it on: "That was Todd, from a phone-box. He wants you to meet him at the usual place – the deserted petrol station, wherever that is."

"What about? I've only just come back from speaking to him."

"How should I know? All he said was he'd got more information since last night. God, I hate all this mystery. I feel a right fool."

Karl popped up from his kitchen stool and kissed her on the nose. "Never mind angel. This sounds promising at least."

"Oh well, thanks for letting me in on it. And don't patronise me."

"Sorry. I've got to dash."

"Well of all the nerve."

"Don't worry, it'll all turn out all right."

"That's what you always say."

"Well believe it then," and he was heading for the door. "Oh, I'll need your car," and swept up her keys from the mantlepiece.

"Karl!"

But he was gone.

When Karl parked Sarah's Micra at the broken-down forecourt a stiff breeze was blowing. Stepping out he pulled his jacket collar up and headed for the cabin.

"Trust Todd not to be on time," he muttered to himself. "It had better be worth it, dragging me out here in the middle of nowhere."

He fell over an old rusted petrol can, and cursing booted it across the yard. Every minute stuck here was wasted time – time when he could be finding a way to Judy. If Todd had nothing to add to that subject, he'd feel the hard edge of Karl's tongue.

By the way, where was he? Karl looked both ways along the road but could see no car. He had spent so much time alone that the solitude was quickly getting to him. It was like the out-station to nowhere. He remembered that horrible dream of his where he was walking along a never ending empty highway, the horizon always receding into nothingness.

Shivering he retreated to the cabin and wrenched open the door. The old counter, cracked and chipped, was still in place, with newspapers, bottles and cartons to indicate the occasional vagrant had found shelter there too.

Bored, he pushed past the counter to see what lay beyond. There was a stockroom and a heavily wedged door. He pushed but could only open it a few inches. Through the gap he could see a broken window and empty room. Curious he pushed harder and forced the weight behind the door to one side.

He edged through the gap he'd made and fell over someone's legs. Scrambling to his feet he looked down: Frank lay there, as lifeless as a sack of potatoes, with a knife in his chest, embedded up to the hilt.

Karl sagged back, gasping, then he went down on his knees, pulling at the knife, fighting with his father's chest to hammer some life into it. But it was hopeless. The knife was somehow stuck and his father was now an inert lump of flesh.

Karl crawled away, and was sick in a corner. His eyes stung with tears. First Gary, now Frank. His family was being stripped away from him, leaving him totally exposed, alone.

163

Then nausea over, he forced himself to return to stand by Frank's body. A few months ago, when he'd thought Frank already dead, he'd shed no tears. Only bitterness and rejection had filled his heart.

But Frank's reappearance and sought for reconciliation had broken down his resistance. He'd started to remember the few good times in his childhood and youth, the sprees he had taken him on. It didn't blot out the misery of being discarded in between, but it compensated a little.

He realised his father had been feckless and under bad influences but had still loved him – when he remembered Karl existed.

And now the only father he'd ever have was dead. All chance of closeness, intimacy was ended. Whatever fresh start his father had sought was lost. Too little, too late. Karl felt an awful sense of waste – of both their lives, deprived of each other.

Who had done this? Then anger burned from his eyes: Todd of course. Todd had resented Frank's return, feared for his own power and safety. They must have fought and Todd in desperation had decided to put the blame on Karl.

The phone call was just a blind, to lure him here so he could be found by the authorities with his dead father. Linked to so many previous deaths, he was made to take the fall.

Todd would have tipped off the police – anonymously of course – to implicate Karl as deeply as possible.

He had to get out and away. But how could he leave his father, discarded on the gravelly floor of an old stock room, in this blitzed hovel?

Feeling guilty as hell, Karl dragged himself away. "Sorry Dad. It's horrible to leave you this way. But what can I do?"

Furious with himself and the whole world he sprinted for the car, and then in it roared away.

As he drove he found it hard to concentrate on the road. The image of Frank's body, butchered and dumped like garbage, kept flashing before his eyes. He felt giddy, sickened, and frightened.

Todd was like some dark loathsome presence, contaminating his world and killing all Karl's loved ones. Karl had to fight back but he needed time to think, and time was running out. It was slipping through his fingers and he had achieved nothing. He was careering to oblivion.

All he could think of was to return to Sarah's flat. Breathless he ran up the stairs and banged on the door.

Sarah's puzzled face appeared as she opened it. "There's no need . . ."

But before she could finish he brushed past her and then slammed the door shut. "Hey, now wait a minute," Sarah began, but then Karl's highly agitated face stopped her. "Karl? What is it?"

Karl was scraping at his hair, tearing at himself. "You wouldn't believe it. Frank's dead. Remember that phone call from Todd?"

Sarah nodded, hypnotised.

"It was a set up. He was sending me to find Frank murdered."

"Karl. You didn't? Tell me."

"Oh yes. There he was, a knife sticking out of his chest. It was horrible. I can't get over it."

"Karl, sit down," and Sarah pulled on his arm. He subsided onto the sofa, and then his head buried in her arms.

"I thought I was tough, but this has done for me. I've never seen anything like it."

"I know, I know. It was too awful for words," Sarah tried to soothe him. "But it's over now. You're safe here with me." But even as she said it, she gave an involuntary shudder. She didn't consider herself brave, and suppose she and Karl were next.

Karl pulled his head up and looked into her eyes. She saw sorrow, terror, and deep pained anger.

"Sarah, if the police come, you've got to tell them I was with you here all the time."

"What?"

"Sarah, Todd's fitted me up. I'll go down for it otherwise."

"Karl, I can't lie for you."

"Why not? You'd be saving my life."

"But I just can't. They wouldn't believe me."

Karl grabbed her by the arm. "Don't give me that. You've got to help me."

"Karl, I love you, but this is wrong. The police will discover that Todd did it."

Karl shook her. "Not with my luck. Get real."

Sarah dragged herself free and stood up. "I don't care, I won't do it. You're trying to drag me into this, and it's all wrong. How do I know you didn't kill Frank?"

Karl's eyes pleaded in desperation. "How can you even think that? Why don't you believe me?"

"Karl, all I know is I won't be used any more. You'd better go. The police may turn up any time."

"You just want to keep out of this, don't you? Not soil your hands."

"It's your dirty business, so yes."

Karl squeezed his hands compulsively. He'd like to make her but he must go now before he was picked up.

"Here are your keys. Remember – I haven't used them."

"Karl. Please leave. Take the keys."

"All right. I'm going. But think of me and what you're doing."

Then he shook his head, and stormed out, longing to take his frustration and anger out on somebody.

Chapter Thirty-five

Karl drove off again in Sarah's car; a wild frenzy gripped him. Everything seemed to be closing in on him. He had one last mission: to exact revenge on Judy and then he was finished, exhausted. He couldn't run any longer.

He sought frantically the motorway exit closest to the open prison where Judy was held. If he could get out of prison he could find a way in. She was probably stretched out in there, thinking she was safe and secure from him. What a shock she'd get when he burst in!

Gripping the wheel tightly he accelerated. He wanted to annihilate time, as in his drug-fuelled rites, and be there, standing over her, retribution at hand. So often he had been accused of murders he had not committed; by a perverse logic this would be one he'd want to be his.

He revelled in the thought that there was no escape for Judy. She was like a butterfly fluttering in a jar. Prison was going to deliver her up to him helpless.

He swung the car off the motorway and drove down picturesque country lanes towards the prison. The bucolic surroundings he surveyed with ironic detachment. Long ago the veneer of country life had been stripped away for him to expose raw hatreds and primitive feuds.

Following the signs, he eventually parked up under an over-arching chestnut tree and got out. From the stile of a farmer's field he could survey the prison. He could see a ditch and a double set of barbed wire fencing. Beyond were long white huts with neat curtains, lined by well-tended flower-beds.

He retreated to the car and settled down to wait for nightfall.

He dosed fitfully but fragmented nightmares of chases and jamming guns destroyed his peace. In between he stretched his legs, but pointless wanderings up and down lanes only made them ache. Action was what he wanted, what he was psyched up for.

"At last," he murmured fervently as darkness, which had seemed never coming, finally settled over the world. From the car he took a torch, rug, and a wheel wrench, which he hid inside his jacket.

Then he moved quickly and silently along the lane and across the field to the prison perimeter. He slithered down into the ditch and listened. Far off across the prison courtyard he could hear subdued voices.

Climbing up the other side he lay flat beneath the barbed wire and kept lookout for a few minutes but there were no patrols.

Then using the blanket to smother the barbed wire he climbed through one fence. He was now in no-man's-land and pressed himself down flat again. If he was seen he was trapped. But soon he felt safe to scramble forward and using the blanket again penetrate the last fence.

He was now through but even more exposed than ever. All he could do was gather up his things and walk normally but quickly across to the first hut.

Opening the end door he slipped through and encountered an inmate carrying some bed linen. "Hey sexy," he whispered and smiled.

The girl jumped then hard apprehension settled across her freckled face.

"Get out of here."

"Hey, don't be like that," he coaxed. "I had to see my girl. I missed her so."

The girl softened, interested. Her eyes took in his good-looking features. "Won't I do?"

"You're beautiful but I've gone crazy for Judy."

Miffed she asked suspiciously, "Judy?"

He described her and then began pleading, "I can't sleep. I just need one night with her. I was so desperate I broke in, to surprise her."

"Well that's a turn up. Usually the girls make arrangements to smuggle their boyfriends in. You like to do things the hard way," and she smirked.

"So come on, be a pal. Where is she?"

The girl let him wait for a moment, savouring her power, and then told him, "Second hut down. Her bed is near the far end I think. Of course you could stay here with me," she added wistfully.

"Sorry," and he blew her a kiss as he retreated out of the door.

"Just my luck, and a live one too," the girl muttered after him.

Karl headed down behind the next hut and then entered by the door at the end. Inside the hut he peered down the aisle. There were partitions between each few beds. Quickly he padded down looking behind each partition in turn.

At the second there was Judy, lying on her bed face upwards blowing smoke rings, her eyes a hard and bitter green. She half jumped up when she saw him. But he pushed her back and drew the wheel wrench from his jacket.

"I'm going to beat your head in."

"Karl. How did you . . ?"

"I broke into prison. Funny how easy it was. Just to see you."

"Well now you're here, put that thing down."

"I've waited months and months for this moment. Let me enjoy it." He seemed to be almost going into a trance.

This was the time he might do it. "Karl!" Judy cried, to bring him out of it. "Stop. You don't want to kill me. You're crazy about me."

"After what you've done to me?"

Judy managed to half sit up. "After all that," she called his bluff defiantly. "You still love me or you wouldn't have taken all this trouble."

"Love you? I hate you. I loathe you with every fibre of my body."

"Hey, now don't overdo it."

"Do you remember the last time? We practically tore each other limb from limb."

"Oh don't exaggerate. Although I did want to punish you."

"Like getting me convicted for murder."

Judy managed to look shame-faced. "That was wrong. Awful."

Karl's face spelled incredulity. "Judy, have you any conception of what you did to me? I could have rotted away the rest of my life in jail."

Judy shook her head angrily. "No, I wouldn't have let that

169

happen."

"Oh yes you would, you callous bitch. If it had worked out between you and Randle."

Judy put her hand to her head. "Don't keep banging away at me Karl. I can't think. And put that wrench down. Where did you get it? Sarah I suppose."

Reluctantly Karl lowered his arm, and lay the weapon close to hand.

"You're right of course, Karl. I'm wicked and now I've lost everything – you, Randle though I didn't want him, my freedom – stuck in here. It's me now facing the prison sentence. Can't you be satisfied? I would be, in your shoes."

"Yes, but you're not me."

Impulsively he held her in his arms, and felt her electric body against his. His mouth seared hers with kisses.

Then he dragged himself back. "What am I doing?"

"What you wanted to do all along. What you came for, though you didn't realise it."

"No I didn't. You're confusing me. I came to kill you."

"Karl you've never killed anyone in your life, and you're not going to start now. You came to get even, to bawl me out. You can't do that to a dead body."

"You're right. I wanted to see you suffer, the way I did."

"Well you have. Here I am cut right down to size. So you can gloat as much as you please."

That terrible thunder which had been building in his head for months seemed to be dissipating. He swayed, light-headed.

"I must sit down. You don't know the half of it. Todd's killed Frank and framed me for it."

"What? That's terrible. Then you shouldn't be here. Get away, fast."

"What's the use?"

"You can bed me before you go, if you want. You deserve at least that," Judy offered.

But as he hesitated she watched him jealously. "Or has Sarah entirely taken over in that department? I'm better."

"Still wicked, eh?"

"Can a leopard change its spots?" she smiled back.

"But I'd forget about being the queen of crime. You've obviously no talent for it."

Judy coloured, tense, and then looked around her. "You're probably right. I don't suppose I was really cut out for it."

"Not with Todd calling the shots."

"That's true," she mused. "Did he shop me?"

"I don't know. Probably. He doesn't want competition."

"No, he only likes whores."

Karl began to feel restless. "I'd better beat it before I get caught."

"How did you get in?"

"Through the barbed wire."

"Oh. Well don't cut yourself getting out. Stay in one piece for me."

"Still after my body?"

"Well you're obviously not after mine."

"Not here, not now."

"Karl, I really am sorry. I messed it all up for us, didn't I?"

"It was the triangle that did for us – you, me and Sarah."

"Yes, Sarah."

"Tell me, for the record. Did you two set a trap for me?"

"My, how imaginative you can be. Well, yes, it may have sort of started like that. But then we both fell for you, and jealousy split us apart." She looked down, bitter and angry. "I suppose I should hate you for that."

"I'm sorry. I never meant to," Karl added.

"No one does – except Todd. Fix him for me Karl and get me out of here. Oh I know I've no right to ask."

"What can I do? Look, there's someone coming."

"Karl, please. I'm desperate."

"I know, I'll think . . . oh I've got to go." He snatched a last kiss, and then ran out of the hut, with Judy's hands reaching out after him.

Chapter Thirty-six

Next morning as Sarah opened the door, with finality Karl pressed the car keys into her hand.

Her eyes widened: "You've seen Judy?"

He nodded, serious, weary.

"And . .?" she daren't ask more, terrified of the answer.

"I didn't kill her, if that's what you're thinking." And Karl burst into the room, all the pent up energy and frustration charging through him. "I meant to. That's why I went. But seeing her there in that shabby dress, on an old cot bed, I hadn't the heart. Not even after all she's done to me. It's clear, it's over. I'm finished with her."

Sarah clung to Karl. "I'm glad. I knew you weren't the sort to go through with it."

"Don't be too sure. If she'd picked a fight, then I might have lost my rag."

Sarah pulled his face down towards her. "But the important thing is you didn't. You're learning. Kiss me."

As they embraced, both began to sense a third presence. "You do get around."

Karl pulled away to see Randle shutting the door carefully behind him.

"What are you doing here?"

"I thought I'd pay you a visit." Randle was wearing a grimy old policeman's trench coat.

"This is my flat and I'm asking you to leave," Sarah told him.

Randle barely spared her a glance. "Be quiet."

Karl was ready, nimble on his feet. "Well?"

"You slept with Judy last night."

172

"What? She's in prison."

"Don't patronise me. You were seen. I have my contacts in there, willing to trade a little information."

"So?"

Randle's face was grey, lined, badly shaven. "Yes, some inmates like turning the knife. She'd told me she was finished with you. I could kill you both."

Karl backed a little, careful now. "As it happens I didn't sleep with my wife. Though that's our business. And we are finished. You want her, you take her."

"While you make up to popsy here?" Randle sneered.

"All right that's enough," and Karl moved to push Randle out.

But Randle was too quick for him. He pulled his old service revolver from his coat pocket.

"Too cocky, that's your trouble. Always ready with a smart answer. Well talk your way out of this one.

Karl moved to cover Sarah. "What's that for?"

Randle pondered, slouching. "It's a moot point. Todd says the police want you for murder."

"I didn't kill my own father. Todd did that."

"You seem very well informed. Why should Todd do that?"

"I don't know. I suppose they had a falling out."

"Or you did. You couldn't stand your father."

"No, that's not true. Well not at the end."

Randle yawned. "Anyway, to be honest I'm not that interested. Except if it would guarantee your conviction."

Karl listened horrified to what seemed to be the ramblings of a sick mind. "Why do you hate me?"

Randle's eyes were grim, levelled at him. "How long have you got? Because you've never done a hard day's work in your life, because you've scrounged and talked your way into the bed of half the women in this county. Because Judy only used me to get back at you. Because you're always in my damned way."

"Because I'm young and you're old," Karl quietly completed for him.

"Old, yes damn it. But not worn out, done-for the way some people think. I have my pride. So maybe I'll gun you down. Resisting arrest."

"And Sarah?"

"Sorry."

173

But he hadn't said the word before Karl had dived at his legs. His arm went up and a shot volleyed into the ceiling.

Then he was lurching backwards, unable to break his fall. Karl was scrabbling to retain his hold and reach for Randle's gun arm. Then he was pounding at Randle's jaw.

Randle writhed in Karl's grasp and brought the gun butt down on Karl's shoulder. Karl howled in pain, and rolled over Randle, who brought the gun down level and fired.

Karl jumped with the force of the explosion, and waited for the sickening feeling in his body to overwhelm him. But nothing happened. He looked down at his thighs, then his chest, but could see no injury.

Not, that is, till he looked at the gaping wound in Randle's right leg.

Randle screamed in agony. "Look. That was for you." And despair shook him.

"Not your lucky day," Karl murmured.

Sarah came and stood over Randle, morbidly fascinated. Then she knelt down and inspected the wound. "I'll get some first-aid," she said efficiently and went to the kitchen.

She returned and patched him up with disinfectant, and bandages.

"I'll ring for an ambulance," she added. As she phoned, Karl watched Randle writhing, uneasy.

When she returned, Karl pulled her to one side. "I can't stay here. Once the police come too I'm cooked. No one will believe Randle shot himself."

"I can tell them the truth."

"They'd think you were lying to protect me. It's no use."

"But Karl, you can't keep on running."

"Then come with me."

"I can't leave Randle. He might bleed to death."

"Then tough. I need you more. Please."

"Karl, I can't. It's impossible. Stay. We'll see it through together."

"No chance. No one ever believes me. I'm not going back to prison. Ever. I'd rather die."

"Karl! Don't, please."

Randle half sat up in deep pain but wearing a lop-sided grin. "What a pair. Can't make your minds up about anything, can you?

174

Pathetic."

"Just stuff it Randle," Karl turned on him.

"Why? What are you going to do? Finish me off."

But Karl turned to ignore him, and faced Sarah again. "You must come. We can start afresh."

"Where? Think Karl."

"I don't know. What does it matter? We'd be together. Help me."

"Karl, what more can I do?"

"So – you're letting me down."

"No. But why can't we do what is right?"

"Oh it's no use talking to you. I'm not getting anywhere. At least Judy has guts. She wouldn't be frightened."

"I'm not. Why are you throwing Judy in my face like this? It's not my fault Randle's shot."

"All right. I can't think straight. It's all going wrong again. I've got to get out."

Randle watched him go, dismissively. "Leaving you in the lurch."

"Oh shut up," and Sarah turned away.

Chapter Thirty-seven

Karl was at the end of his rope. Everything seemed to be blowing up in his face. All the people he had known and trusted, loved, were dead or had let him down. He was on that long, lonely highway of his dreams. There was nowhere he could call home.

He'd been out there too long, 'getting lost for a while'. He didn't recognise his old self – the wayward spirit forever on the move from one woman to another. The future appeared shrouded in mystery.

And then he remembered a woman of dark eyes and exotic appeal: Gloria. How could he have not recognised that she was the true original, and her daughters were pale imitations? She was twice the woman they would ever be, large-hearted and generous. Jealous too, but always there for him when he needed her.

How often in the last few months had she offered every sort of help? She'd laid herself on the line for him, and he'd spurned her.

He must have been mad to throw all that away. Maybe it was too late. Perhaps she had had enough of him.

Whatever, he must find out now. His head cleared and he looked about him. He must cut across town to the ring road. He'd try and pick up a lift to the village.

As he waved thank you to the lorry driver, he gazed up at the long winding incline into the village through those massive boulders from a pre-historic age. He began toiling upwards, wondering what reception he would get from the villagers, never mind Gloria. Last time they had tried to run him out of the village, and nearly killed him.

As he emerged over the ridge and began the descent between the farmhouses and down among the village shops, he felt exposed, helpless. Should they all emerge and surround him, he was done for.

But the street was deserted. Were they watching him, secretly, behind lace curtains? On he plodded telling himself to calm down. They'd probably forgotten all about him. Still it would do no harm to hurry out of danger's way, and he increased his pace.

Up through the end of the village centre he hastened without drawing attention to himself. There on the bend was Gloria's bungalow. How often had he taken for granted the comfortable, elegant furnishings, its sun-soaked patio? He'd come and gone as he pleased, never doubting that he was always welcome.

What would be his reception now? There was only one way to find out and he rang the bell.

Minutes later Gloria appeared, flushed from gardening in a huge orange floral smock and long brown skirt and sandals.

"Karl!" she rocked on her heels then threw herself upon him. "Am I glad to see you."

They were kissing and hugging with total abandon. "What will the neighbours think?" Karl smirked.

"Sod the neighbours. Come here you sight for sore eyes."

Once inside Gloria led him through into the living-room, and they were soon entwined on the couch.

"Hey, let me draw breath."

"Never," and she tickled him.

"What a way to go," and he collapsed in mock expiry.

"I'll soon bring you back to life," and Gloria pressed herself against him.

Then she stood up and stretched out her hand. He smiled and nodded, and they made their way to the bedroom.

Afterwards, as they lay side by side, Gloria began: "So where did you spring from?"

Karl rubbed his eyes. "It's a long story. I finally came to my senses and realised it was you all along. Judy and Sarah were just distractions."

"It's certainly a weird triangle," and Gloria rose, pulling on a purple robe. "What do you intend to do? Divorce Judy?"

"I suppose so."

"Suppose?"

Karl pulled himself together. "Well of course, yes. But with her banged up in prison it's not that easy."

Gloria turned on her heels. "Listen, if I take you back, it's on my terms. No little bits on the side, particularly my own daughters. I won't put up with it."

Karl grabbed at her hand. "Of course not. I never two-timed you, ever."

Gloria snorted. "I'll have to take your word for it. But don't say you weren't tempted. You've got to learn to keep your loins under control."

"My what?" he laughed.

"Your . . . you know," and Gloria buckled into laughter too and collapsed onto the bed. "You're terrible you are," she teased him.

"No more terrible than you, dragging me into the bed before I'd barely crossed the threshold."

"Me! You scamp. You'll pay for that," and she leapt upon him again, tearing off her robe.

Later, exhausted, they both emerged into the kitchen for sustenance. As they thoughtfully munched croissants and drank a cafetiere of coffee, Gloria debated and then said, "It was terrible about Frank."

"You heard?"

"Of course. The papers were full of it. The man back from the dead finally meets his end. It was creepy."

"He was murdered. Todd killed him."

Gloria dropped her food. "Todd! So that bastard did it. Mind you, he always resented Frank coming back. But Todd was crazy to think that Frank was muscling in on his operation. Frank had given up on all that. You were his priority now."

"I know. That's the tragedy of it, just as we were becoming reconciled and getting to know each other. I'll never forgive Todd, as long as I live."

"Me too."

Karl banged down his mug and knife. "In fact, thinking about it, I'm going to finish that man once and for all. He's ruined too many lives. Gary and Frank are dead. It's got to stop."

"What are you going to do?"

"A deal with the police, if I can, he's got it coming. Did you know he betrayed Judy to the police, because she was going freelance?"

"Todd would sell his own mother."

"Well no more. I'm putting a stop to him once and for all."

"Go to it."

"Yes – now where's that phone?"

Chapter Thirty-eight

Karl stood opposite Todd who sat at his desk, pen poised, amazed at Karl's audacity. The room was decrepit with battered green filing cabinets, a heavily scored desk, and musty emulsioned walls.

"Is all this a blind or does crime not pay as well as I thought?"

"You should know."

"But I don't. I'm an amateur compared with you. You have so many talents – blackmail, robbery, murder."

"All right, that's it. Out. I've put up with all I'm going to take from you."

Karl lurched forward, head jutting over the desk. "Oh no, I'm just getting started and you're going to listen to every word."

"Why? Who's going to make me?" and Todd began to drag his bulk up out of his chair.

"Sit down," and Karl thrust him back.

Todd scowled, angrily.

"People have always been too afraid of you to speak their minds. Well I'm not."

"Oh and what makes you so different? Dutch courage or have you forgotten all the jobs you pulled for me?"

"We made use of each other, I don't deny it. But I was desperate."

"So?"

"Your power is all used up. I'm turning Queen's Evidence. You're going down for everything – the robberies, Frank's murder."

"You'd shop me?"

"Without a moment's hesitation. You're a bloated parasite and

I'll get a big cheer from everyone."

"Who put you up to this? You're not bright enough to have thought it all up for yourself."

"No one."

"Judy's in prison, Sarah would never have the bottle, so that leaves Gloria."

"Why bring up Gloria? It's you we're concerned about. I want to relish watching you squirm until the police arrive."

"No: let's stick with Gloria. She's the key. Why do you think she's as keen as you to send me down?"

"I don't know – because she loathes you like everyone else."

Todd brushed the insult aside with his hand. "You're not catching on. She has a special reason."

"Why? What have you been up to?"

"Not me, her. If you want to save her you'll keep your mouth shut about me."

"Is this a riddle?"

"No, but I'll make it simple for you. If I go down, I'm taking Gloria with me."

"You've got something on Gloria?"

"At last: light dawns."

Karl leant back. "I don't care. Whatever it is."

"You'll care when you know."

"So Gloria has a past. Haven't we all? It's no good Todd. Nothing you can say will shock me."

"She's a killer."

"What!"

"She killed all those women. She was madly jealous of any woman who looked at you."

"Rubbish. How could you know all this? Why haven't you spoken before?"

"Gloria came to me. She was manic, terrified she'd be found out and sent to Broadmoor or worse."

"She asked you to protect her? You blackmailed her. I might have known. I bet you drugged her first and then she confessed."

"Well, do we have a deal?"

Karl was ashen. "You ask me that? You tell me Gloria's a murderess and then calmly discuss business. What kind of man are you?"

"A survivor, that's all, getting by, like everyone else. Now take

181

it or leave it."

"I can't think. It must be all lies. Maybe you planted the idea in Gloria's head and she's innocent."

"You believe that? Ask her. Then you'll both be in it together."

"You're evil, you know that. Trading on people's misery."

"Spare me. Come on, how does it feel to be sleeping with a murderess?"

Karl lunged at Todd but was too late. "Wait till I get my hands on you."

Todd grinned. "I'm always one step ahead of you, remember that. Now go and see your lady friend. We'll have a deal, you'll see. And you'll have Gloria – for life. What a prospect. I pity you." And he dismissed Karl with a wave of his hand.

Chapter Thirty-nine

Gloria was standing in the middle of the living-room, a voluminous purple smock shimmering around her. She wore a gold, saw-tooth necklace and a bangle round her wrist.

"Well. Did you see Todd carted away? I wish I'd been there."

"No. There's been an unexpected twist."

"Oh Karl, you didn't let him get away?"

"I had to see you first."

"Me!" and she moved evasively towards the window, straightening the curtains. "You didn't need to check with me. You know how I feel – send the old bastard down for life. In fact hanging would be too good for him."

"You're a killer," Karl interposed in a quiet, menacing tone.

"What did you say? Don't be preposterous."

"Todd knows you killed them all."

"Then he's raving mad. I don't go round killing people. You don't believe this crazy story?"

"I have to know."

"Well now you do. I've never been so insulted; in fact insulted is nothing to what I feel. Revolted, sick."

"All right, I get the message. But you know Todd, into everything."

"Not this. Can't you see he was desperate, lying to buy time, and you fell for it?" She came forward, and gazed straight at him.

Karl felt his resolution oozing away. After all, he only had Todd's word for any of it.

Gloria turned on her heel and then plumped down in the sofa, as if holding court. "You know what I think: Todd was diverting suspicion from himself. I don't know why I didn't think of it before. He hated to see you seducing all those women who wouldn't give him the time of day. So he took revenge and killed them."

Karl listened and stared. It all made sense. Todd wouldn't scruple at murder: after all, he'd killed Frank. It would be typical of Todd to accuse Gloria as a smoke screen.

Karl was shame-faced. "I'm sorry Gloria, truly. I've been a fool. Only he threatened to send you down and I suppose I panicked. Too much has been happening lately. I can't tell what's true any more. I don't know how I could have thought it of you for a second."

"What do you want me to say? That I forgive you? You'll have a long wait."

"Gloria, I was out of my head. I didn't know what to think."

"And what about me? You turn up out of nowhere. We fall in love again, just like before and then you accuse me of this. It's horrible."

"I know, unforgivable. Try and forget it. I had an aberration. It was Todd, as usual, manipulating me. But I'll get him for it."

Gloria nodded towards the drinks cabinet. "Please, pour me my usual. I need it."

Karl brought a gin over to her and took a beer himself. "We'll feel better after these," he promised her.

The drinks seemed to help to dispel the ominous atmosphere. After a while it was almost possible to believe it had all never happened.

Gloria went and dug out some cold meat and cheese from the fridge, and they had a picnic on the carpet like they used to. Dry white wine frothed up in glasses and they began to relax in each other's company.

"You are crazy," and Gloria stroked Karl's head.

"I know," he confessed. "I've been wrong about everything from the start. If I'd stuck with you it would have all been all right."

"Maybe it's too late."

"No it's not. We can make a go of it now my head's clear and Todd will be out of the way."

"Don't keep mentioning his name. Let's forget him."

Karl lay back on her lap. "You're right. He's history. It's you and me with the future now."

184

Gloria dragged her hand through his hair. "We could have an even better one," she replied enigmatically.

"What are you smiling about? Come on, out with it. I hate secrets."

"Well, I suppose it's all in the family. When Frank and I were close again recently he told me about a cache of valuables. He can't use it any more. So why shouldn't we enjoy it?"

Karl tensed and sat up. "I want no part of it."

"Yes, but listen Karl. The haul's doing no one any good just lying there. And it's too late to return it all."

"Leave it where it is," and Karl jumped up. "I mean it Gloria. Frank's crimes brought nothing but grief, and ruined our lives. No good can come from it."

"Good God, I think you've caught Frank's morality. Before he died he was full of remorse, and sanctimonious too."

"Well maybe he'd learnt something before it was too late."

Gloria grabbed at Karl. "This is important Karl. Are you with me on this or against me?"

Karl stared into her eyes baffled. "What does it matter? We have each other. We don't need Frank's loot."

"I do. You try bringing up two daughters on next to nothing. This bungalow is mortgaged to the hilt. I don't want to spend the rest of my life in poverty."

"You won't."

"And what is your profession? Handyman, sometime photographer. I'm not keeping you, like your other lady friends."

Karl flared up. "No woman has kept me. I don't live off women. I pay my way."

"Oh yes." Gloria was scornful. "I'd like some evidence." Then she changed again: "But don't you see it doesn't have to be like this. Think of it as a sort of bequest to us from Frank to start all over."

"But it's tainted with the past. We can't buy happiness that way."

"Then what do you suggest we live on?"

"I don't know. Stop badgering me."

"Oh this is getting us nowhere."

Gloria gave him a furious look and downed her glass of wine. "Don't let's talk any more. My head is spinning. We'll ruin everything if we carry on like this."

185

"Your head! You should feel mine. Truce?"

Then he sprawled down, with his back to a chair, and stared at the broken remnants of their picnic. If only he hadn't drunk so much.

Burning, burning: the words seemed to pound at his brain, to wake him up. He leant on one elbow and felt awful nausea, the room spinning. Fire seemed to spurt up all around the room. He turned to look around but every movement of his head was torture. Then fire graced up a curtain and he knew the horror was upon him.

Gloria weaved in front of him, ecstatic. "Gloria! help me out of here."

"It's no use. Todd knew the truth. You would have found out eventually."

"Gloria, please."

"I was playing for time. If the police came they'd have found out everything. Frank's hoard is buried under the patio. All we had to do was dig it up."

"Gloria, never mind all that. You can't leave me here to burn to death."

Gloria looked down at him pityingly. "I'm sorry, Karl. You're great in bed but you have too many scruples. Why couldn't you take the money and we could have gone away together?"

Karl was coughing and suffering from heatstroke. He stretched out his hand. "Please!"

The cracking sound of fire eating into wood, the beating heat, then choking smoke were all advancing into the room. Karl tried to stir himself, ignore the nausea, just move, but his body seemed paralysed.

Gloria hovered over him. "You've caused me such suffering, do you know that? All those lovers. Wanting them and not me. Even my own daughters. But I couldn't kill them. They are my flesh and blood. Better you should die instead. Then I'll be free at last."

Karl realised his appeals to her were hopeless, ignored. Instead he began inching along the carpet, dragging his useless body forward.

Gloria simply watched him. Then she moved to block his way.

186

"Oh no, you're going nowhere."

Karl reached out and yanked her ankle. Down she toppled and then he was squeezing past her, blurred eyes fixed on the front door.

The flames were roaring in his ears, the heat was an enveloping blanket, but still he powered on inch by inch.

Then he heard a terrible scream from behind him. Looking back, he saw a snake of flame licking Gloria's smock. Frantically she beat at the flames, tore at her smock, terror distorting her face.

Karl turned away and pressed on. The door was only yards now, if he could just make it. His head was swimming and his limbs felt like rope. He mustn't be weak, no matter what he must escape. Gloria mustn't win.

As the inferno behind him reached a crescendo he scrabbled at the door handle. Frantic seconds followed and then he fell out onto the front step.

As he lay there, gasping for air, an explosion rent the house putting an end to Gloria's torment.

Chapter Forty

Karl paused and gazed at the now familiar barbed-wire earth works and the prison huts beyond. It seemed an appalling risk but then what was the alternative? That lonely highway still stretched ahead of him for ever. Or he could restore a connection with the woman he had married.

That thought spurred him on and he circled unobtrusively to a corner where the barbed wire converged. Using an old rug to insulate his body from the wire, he wriggled inwards.

Then he struggled across the earth, scratched by thistles and dandelions, till he faced the second wire. Then he lay down and waited, panting. He hated this exposed feeling as if searchlights were about to freeze him in their beam and dogs set on him.

"Been watching too many war movies," he muttered to himself.

All the same, if a patrol located him he was trapped against the wire. His retreat was cut off, and there being no room for manoeuvre made him edgy.

Then he saw a figure moving towards him. He tried to make it out across the darkening, purple sky but it moved too quickly. He bit his lip, torn between hope and anxiety, his heart pounding as the figure was rapidly upon him.

Then she sprawled down in front of the wire separating them: Judy.

"I got your message. What a place to pick," she spluttered picking bits of grass and earth out of her mouth.

"I couldn't risk going to the huts again, not after they refused to let me see you."

"Anyway, what's so urgent? I thought we'd said everything."

Karl looked at her, in her muddied pinafore dress, unsuspecting. Her hair was a black swathe across her face, a dark shadow.

"You'd better hear it from me. Gloria's dead."

Judy blinked then twisted in incomprehension. "What are you talking about? Mother is as strong as an ox. She'll outlive us all. She threatens to."

"I mean it Judy. I saw it happen. She went berserk, set fire to the bungalow and died in the flames."

As he saw horror flash across her features, in anguish he went on: "I'm sorry, maybe I should have spared you the details. But you would have to know eventually."

"You saw it? What were you doing there? How could you let it happen?"

Karl inched forward. It was terrible trying to talk of such things through the separation of barbed wire.

"She drugged me. I was supposed to die in the inferno. But she was careless with a petrol can, and I crawled clear with only seconds to spare. I'm lucky to be alive."

Judy put her head down in the earth, bitter, confused, guilty. Then she emerged, eyes smarting with tears. "I can't take all this in. She tried to kill you? Why?"

Realising that the time had come, he told Judy all about Gloria.

Judy stared at him, incredulous. "My mother was a serial killer?"

Quietly but in a tough relenting tone Karl responded: "She told me. Todd had warned me. At first she denied it, then when I was drugged and helpless she revelled in it. You and Sarah came within a hair's breadth of the same fate."

Judy tore back her hair which was falling over her face, smothering her. "Karl, if all this is some trick to get me on your side, I'll see you in hell."

Karl edged forward and strained through the wire, reaching with his fingers till they were inches from hers.

"Judy, I wouldn't have the heart to do that to you, here. I swear to you on my father's grave, every word I have told you is the truth."

Judy gazed back at his earnest, passionate face. She saw the taut muscles, the bone-aching weariness around the eyes, the pleading look. He'd never given his whole being to her like that

189

before. "My God Karl, what you've been through."

"Never mind all that. Do you believe me?"

"Yes, I do. I'm convinced. What now?"

With a super-human effort, Karl stretched his body across the wire, ignoring the barbs searing him and grasped her hand.

"That's all that matters. That you believe me, trust me in what I have to do."

"What can you do?"

"Start afresh and be a proper husband to you."

"Now?"

"Is there a better time? I'm crazy about you. You're beautiful even in the dirt here. You light up the world for me. I want to wait for you, be here for you."

"What, here, in a muddy corner of a prison field?" Judy joked, gripping his fingers tight.

"If that's what it takes, yes. I know I've no track record of dependability . . ."

"No."

". . . but I'll stick with this and see it through. I love you."

Judy gazed at him wryly, perplexed.

"What am I going to do with you? Where has all this come from of a sudden?"

Karl looked embarrassed. "It doesn't sound like me, does it?"

"I think that's a good thing. Maybe I should break with my past, too." Suddenly she gripped his hand hard, suspicious. "This isn't some wind-up to pay me back?"

"No Judy. I want the chance to make a future with you."

Judy grinned. "Why not?"

"Let's get lost, but together. Then we'll always know where we are."